Black Dirt

Nell Leyshon is an award-winning playwright,
with work broadcast on Radio 3 and Radio 4 and published
by Oberon Books. She was brought up in Glastonbury
and lives in Bournemouth. *Black Dirt* is her first novel.

NELL LEYSHON

Black Dirt

PICADOR

First published 2004 by Picador

This edition published 2005 by Picador
an imprint of Pan Macmillan Ltd
Pan Macmillan, 20 New Wharf Road, London N1 9RR
Basingstoke and Oxford
Associated companies throughout the world
www.panmacmillan.com

ISBN 0 330 42640 0

1 3 5 7 9 8 6 4 2

A CIP catalogue record for this book is available from
the British Library.

Typeset by IntypeLibra, Ltd
Printed and bound in Great Britain by
Mackays of Chatham plc, Chatham, Kent

All Pan Macmillan titles are available from www.panmacmillan.com
or from Bookpost by telephoning 01624 677237

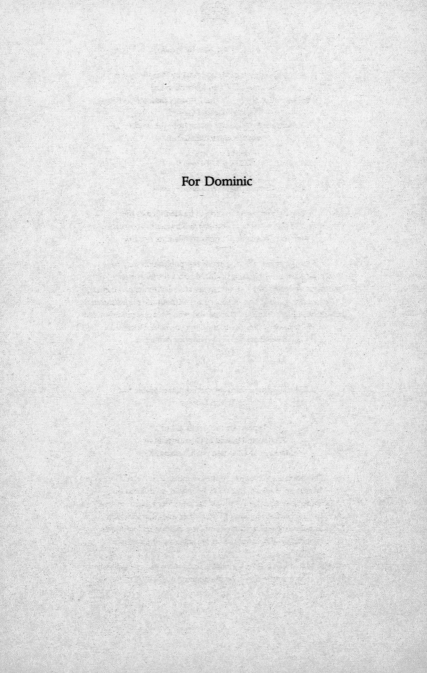

For Dominic

Topsoil

Margaret stood up from the wooden chair. She stretched, then rubbed the small of her back with both hands, walked to the window and looked out at the floods.

A door opened and closed downstairs, and a tap ran.

Margaret turned the curled handle of the window and tried to open it to let a bit of air in, but the wood had swollen from the rain.

Through the glass, she could see the willow. Its small silver buds, bare branches, black from the rain.

Downstairs the tap stopped and there was silence for a while.

Margaret yawned and pushed her hair behind her ears. It was getting dark in the room, but she didn't like to turn the light on. Not yet.

She looked across at the bed. His thin hands resting on the covers. The drip from one of them, the tube leading up to the bag on the metal stand.

The tap from downstairs again. A cupboard door slamming.

'Margaret.'

'I thought you were asleep,' she said.

'Is there any water?'

'Course.'

She walked over to him. Picked up the glass of water from

3

the bedside table and held it to his mouth; he took one small sip, swallowed, then shook his head when she offered more. She replaced the glass, turned on the bedside light.

'Good to be home?'

He looked round the room. 'Yeh.'

Margaret smiled. 'Good.'

'Better than there,' Frank said. 'Never leave you alone there.'

'No. Well, they have to look after you.' Margaret straightened the counterpane, picked up the glass. She dried the bottom of it on her trousers, wiped the water mark it had left on the bedside table, then put it back.

'And you can't sleep there. Soon as you sleep they wake you up. Sticking things in you.'

'Well, you're home now.'

Frank nodded.

Margaret moved to the end of the bed, stood fiddling with the brass knob on the corner of the bedstead.

'You will stay for a bit?' Frank asked. 'Only I don't know if we can manage.'

'You know I will, Dad,' Margaret said. She picked up the small case by the door, placed it on the bottom of the bed.

'Where's Brian?' Frank asked.

'Downstairs with George.'

'With George?'

'Yeh, with George. Look, you're bound to get a bit confused, you know, with all they're giving you.'

'I'm not confused. I know where I am.'

Margaret opened her mouth to speak. Closed it again. Undid the suitcase and took out two pairs of pyjamas, which she laid in the top drawer of the chest.

'I'm not going back there,' he said.

'No.' She placed the slippers under the bed. Put the sponge bag by the door to take through to the bathroom.

4

'Not ever going back.'

'I know.' She felt the sharpness in her voice and told herself to sit down, take a breath. She closed the case and pushed it under the bed, next to the slippers. Sat down.

'All that fussing on.'

'They were just looking after you.'

'I'm a grown man. Didn't need all that.'

Another deep breath. Then, 'How you feeling, anyway?'

'Bit better. Yeh, I reckon I feel a bit better.'

'Well, that's good. Good you're feeling all right.'

'Not all right. I said better.'

'Right.'

'I'll be up and about soon.'

She looked at him as he lay in bed. Say nothing, she told herself.

'So,' he said. 'George is downstairs.'

'Yeh.'

'How was he, without me?'

'He was all right.'

'Spec he missed me.'

'Course he did, but I looked after him well. And Brian was good with him.'

'Spec he's glad I'm home.'

'Yeh.'

She looked at the window. Dark now. Just the reflection of the room. 'Dad,' she said, 'the nurse'll be here tomorrow morning to see to the drugs and that. Give you a wash.'

'Don't need no nurse.'

'And the doctor's coming.'

'I seen enough of doctors for a lifetime.'

'Well, they're coming. You agreed.'

'That was before.'

'You have no choice, Dad.'

5

Frank struggled to sit up. 'I have got a choice. If I don't want them here . . .' He started to cough.

Margaret took his arm, stacked the pillows behind him, one flat, the other two at angles to support him.

'You have to take it easy. Don't go getting yourself worked up.'

She helped him lean back gently against the pillows. There was sweat on his face and his breathing was laboured. 'You okay?' she asked.

He nodded.

'Just try and take it easy.'

He looked away, at the window.

'I've made you some soup,' she said. 'Will you try and eat it?'

'A bit, maybe.'

She saw his hand feel along the bed until it found the button. He held it for a second, then pressed. Liquid flowed from the bag on the stand, down through the tube, into his arm.

Later he opened his eyes and looked round the room, at the window, the four squares of glass, the dark outside.

'You all right?' Margaret in the doorway, a tray in her hands.

He nodded and his head felt heavy.

'I've brought you the soup.' She placed the tray on the table, pulled the chair up close and sat down.

'What is it?' he asked.

'Carrot.'

'My carrots used to love the soil here.'

'Yeh.'

'It was the peat they loved. All that peat got in the topsoil.'

'I know.' Margaret dipped the spoon into the soup. As she lifted it out, some of the orange liquid slopped back into the bowl.

'You ought to grow some,' Frank said.

'It's finding time.'

'George, he used to love helping me out there.'

Margaret smiled. 'That time he pulled them all up.'

Frank laughed. 'Daft bugger.'

'Dunno how you managed not to get cross with him.'

'Oh, you can't get cross with George.' Frank shook his head. 'Not George.'

Margaret looked at the soup. 'You gonna try this, then?'

Frank nodded. Margaret held the spoon out towards his mouth. 'Here.'

As he opened his mouth, the white spit at the corners of his lips stretched then snapped. Margaret tried not to look. Frank sipped at the soup and swallowed.

'Is it okay?'

'Doesn't taste of much.'

Margaret filled the spoon again. 'Spec the medicine messes up the taste buds.'

'Used to taste of something, my carrots.'

She took a breath. 'Well, this is all we got now. Come on.'

He took another sip. Soup dribbled down his chin and Margaret reached for a piece of kitchen roll from the tray, went to wipe his mouth.

'I'm not a baby.'

'You do it, then,' she said.

He wiped his mouth, the movement of his hand dragging the tube across the bed, then handed Margaret the screwed-up piece of kitchen roll. She offered him more soup, but he shook his head.

'You had enough?'

'George coming up to see me?' he asked.

'He's with Brian. They're icing a cake we made.'

He smiled. 'That figures. What colour's he got mixed up?'

7

'Green,' Margaret said. 'C'you manage a little more?'

'I'm not really hungry.'

'No.' She put the spoon back in the soup. 'Well, it doesn't matter. I can warm it up later in the microwave.'

'You wanna watch those microwaves,' Frank said.

Margaret placed the bowl of soup on the tray.

'You don't wanna go trusting them.'

'What d'you reckon they do to you?'

Frank shook his head. 'Cook you from the inside.'

Margaret smiled. 'That's what they do to food, not people.'

'It's not right.'

'They been around ages.'

'You just wait,' Frank said. 'You'll all see.'

'Right,' Margaret said. She looked down at her lap and saw a drop of cake mixture that had fallen on her trousers. She licked her finger and rubbed at the stain, but it made it worse.

Frank looked at the fireplace. The oak mantle. 'We used to cook on that fire,' he said. 'That time the floods got in here. Stuck up here for weeks, we was.'

'You must've got bored.'

'Went out in the boat.' Frank smiled. 'Had to go out the window, down the ladder.'

'Floods are bad now.'

'One of the worst.'

'We were lucky to get you back here,' Margaret said.

'I couldn't have stayed there.'

'No.'

Margaret stared at the fireplace. 'That was the best bit about being ill, the fire.'

'Yeh.'

'I mean, you know, when I was little,' she said.

'I lit one for your mother when George was born.'

Margaret stood up, walked around the bed.

'It rained the day he was born.'

Margaret bent down. The fireplace was dusty inside; the firebrick had a crack in it from top to bottom.

'And the day I was born?' she asked. 'Did it rain then?'

There was a silence for a while, then Frank laughed gently. 'It rained so much the day George was born I thought it'd never stop.'

Margaret nodded to herself. She walked back and picked up the tray. Went to leave.

'You going?' Frank asked.

'I got a lot to do, Dad.'

'Right,' he said. 'I'll call if I need you.'

'I'm sure you will.' She balanced the tray and opened the door, left it ajar.

A few minutes later, George came in the room.

'You're home.'

'Yep. I'm home.'

'Margaret said you were.'

George closed the door and the latch settled in the keep. He pulled the chair up to the bed. Sat down.

'I made a cake.'

'Margaret told me.'

George looked round the room. He crossed then uncrossed his legs. Clapped his hands, rubbed them on his trousers. 'So you're home,' he said.

'I am.'

'And you ain't going away again.'

A pause, then, 'No. I'm staying here now.'

George smiled slowly. 'Good.' He clapped his hands again and rubbed at his grey hair.

'That a new jumper you got, George?'

George plucked at the wool, pulled the sleeves over his hands.

'Margaret got it.'

'Looks like a good one.'

'Yeh,' George said. 'Warm enough.'

'Every man needs a warm jumper.'

'It's been raining,' George said. 'While you was away. Margaret said it'd never stop, it rained so much. Brian got the boat out, had to go everywhere in it. Shops and Glastonbury and everything.'

'I came home in it.'

George looked at Frank. 'Did you?'

'How else was I gonna get home?'

George smiled. 'Oh yeh.'

'Spec you liked it in the boat with Brian.'

'Yeh.'

'You like the old boat.'

'I do.' George stared at the wall. 'Dad?'

'Yeh.'

'D'you know, I'd like to be a boat.'

Frank smiled.

George stood up and walked to the window, then back. He sat down and crossed his legs again, his trousers riding up, showing his bare white ankles. He had his favourite shoes on and the stitching had gone, so the sole gaped open. 'See, thing is,' George said, 'if you were a boat, you'd know what you were.'

'Spose you would. You're gonna need new shoes soon.'

George shook his head. 'Don't make these ones no more.'

'You'll have to find some others you like.'

'I don't like no others.'

'They're only shoes.'

George lifted up his foot. He pulled the sole, saw where

the stitching had rotted. 'Reckon Margaret could put some glue in?'

'Maybe.'

'Maybe I'll ask her.'

'You ain't got no socks on,' Frank said.

'No. I gone off socks.'

'Any reason for it?'

George shrugged. 'My feet don't like them any more. Used to, but they don't now.'

'Didn't Margaret tell you to put some on?'

'She tried. She says she's staying for a bit, Dad.'

'She is. It's just while I ain't right.'

'And she'll go when you're better?'

Frank nodded. 'Yeh. You like her being here?'

George thought for a second. 'It's all right,' he said. 'I like Brian.'

'But you missed me.'

'Course I did. You're my dad.'

'I am. And I'm home now.'

'You are.'

George picked up the water from the bedside table, swallowed, placed the empty glass back. 'I like a drink of water,' he said.

'I was telling Margaret about the day you were born.'

'When was that?'

'You know when it was. When's your birthday?'

A pause.

'The second day in March.'

'The first. March the first.'

'Soon, my birthday is. Margaret said I'm gonna be fifty.' George leant forward and stroked the counterpane. 'Is fifty old?'

'No, fifty's not old.'

'Oh,' George said. 'Good.'

They sat in silence for a while, then, 'I told Margaret how I lit a fire in here the day you were born.'

'I helped you light a fire there once.'

'That's right.'

'We burned that stuff you used to dig.'

'Peat turves.'

'That's them. Brown, they are.'

'Depends,' Frank said. 'Can be black, light brown. Depends how deep you dig.'

George scratched his nose.

'The deeper you dig the older it is, see.'

'Is peat older than me?'

'Christ, yeh. Peat's older than anything. Older than Jesus.'

'The foot-washer.'

Frank laughed. 'Yeh. That's the one. What I used to like, George, was when you cut down into the head, you'd see the layers. All the colours. Topsoil right down to the bedrock.'

'I don't dig peat,' George said.

'No.'

'I go to the centre in Glastonbury.'

'You been while I was away?'

George shook his head. 'Brian said I didn't have to. What with the floods and that. Will I be in trouble?'

Frank smiled. 'You're all right. They wouldn't expect you this weather.'

'No,' George said. 'Course they wouldn't.'

'You do like it there, mind?'

George nodded. 'S'all right. Can't stay here all the time, can I?'

'No. You'd be bored.'

'I wouldn't mind for a bit though. You know, stopping in with you.'

'It'll be a few days before you go back. What with the floods.'

'Oh. Good.'

'So where did you go in the boat with Brian?'

'We went and fed some cattle on the island.'

'Took them food, did you?'

'Yeh. Brian did it for Ivor. He rang and asked if he would. See,' George said, 'if you don't feed them, they die.'

'That's right.'

'Same as us. If we don't eat, we die. We got to drink too.'

'Cattle must've had a lot to drink, what with the floods,' Frank said.

'That's right. Brian said there wasn't no need to take them some drinks.'

'They'll have drunk the floodwater.'

'Yeh.' George laughed. 'Shame they couldn't drink it all, eh? Mind, then I'd have to go to the centre, and I wanna stay here with you.'

Frank smiled.

They sat in silence for a while, then, 'I made a cake.'

'I know. You told me.'

'Oh, I told you, did I? I do like a cake.'

'I know,' Frank said.

'Chocolate, it was. I done icing too.'

'Don't tell me. I'll guess what colour.'

George clapped. Rubbed his hair with both hands.

'You did it red.'

'No.' George shook his head.

'Maybe blue,' Frank said, 'you got a new thing of blue colouring not so long ago.'

George stamped his feet, then licked his finger and polished the toes of his shoes.

'No. Not blue.' Frank paused. 'Got it. You did it green. You iced it green. Well?'

George clapped his hands. 'How d'you know that?'

'Oh, I'm a clever bugger.'

'And me,' George said. 'I'm a clever bugger too.'

'You are, George. You are.'

Neither spoke for a few moments. Then, 'You never used to be yellow.'

'No.'

'Your eyes.' George pointed at his own eyes. 'All yellow.' He threaded his fingers together and bent his hands backwards. His finger joints clicked. 'Dad,' he said, then stopped.

'Go on.'

George shook his head.

'Come on. Tell me.'

George stared at his favourite crack, which ran right across the ceiling, dividing it in half.

'Come on.'

'I didn't like it with you gone.'

'I know.'

George looked down at the floor, ran his toe along the line of the floorboard.

'I'm home now, Georgie.'

'And you won't go away again?'

Frank shook his head. 'No.'

George reached over and tapped the tube where it came out from under the bandage on Frank's hand. 'What's that?'

'Medicine,' Frank said. 'They put it straight in my body.'

'Oh,' George said. 'Medicine makes you better.'

'That's right.'

'Yeh. Medicine makes you better.'

Silence for a while. Then Frank said, 'Will you call Margaret for me?'

14

George laughed. 'Did you know Wednesdays are yellow? Like you.'

'Call Margaret.'

'Sundays are red and one of the days is purple but I can't remember which one.'

'Please.'

George stood up and went to the door, called Margaret's name. He sat back down. 'Is there a day called a Friday?'

Frank moved his hand but couldn't find the button.

A door downstairs and feet on the stairs. Margaret in the doorway.

'Water.' Frank's fingers still feeling for the button.

'I drank the water,' George said. 'I did.'

'You mustn't,' Margaret said. 'Dad needs it.' She gave the glass to George. 'Go on, go and get some more.' George took the glass and left the room.

Margaret stood by the bed. 'You want to lie down?'

Frank shook his head.

She moved the button so he could reach it easily. 'I can tell him not to come up. You know, if you need some quiet.'

'No.'

'Okay. Whatever.'

He turned his head away, looked at the wall.

'Does it hurt?'

Nothing.

George came back in and Margaret took the glass, raised it to Frank's lips. He swallowed.

'You gonna get up, Dad?' George asked.

'Soon,' Frank said. 'I'll be up soon.'

Margaret put the glass down.

A pause.

'Come on,' she said. 'Dad needs some quiet now.' She took George's arm and led him out of the room.

Frank found the button, pressed it and closed his eyes.

~

'Frank.'

He opened his eyes. The room was dark. Night.

'Frank. Come on. Father's waiting.'

The door closing. The sound of feet down the stairs.

Frank pushed back the covers, reached for his short trousers and shirt. He walked across the floorboards, opened the door, stepped onto the stone circular staircase. His hand followed the curved wall of the stairway and he edged carefully forward, his feet finding each step. The gas lamp downstairs lit the last few stairs and he jumped down onto the flagstone floor. Father stood by the table. 'Get your boots on,' he whispered.

Frank went into the scullery and pushed his bare feet into his boots. Followed Father out.

Iris stood outside in the dark.

'D'you know where we're going?' Frank asked.

'He won't tell me.'

It was warm, even in the open air, in the thick of night. There was a moon, nearly full, and they could see their way easily as they started off after Father, passing the hen house and the vegetable patch, crossing the railway-sleeper bridge over the rhyne which bordered their land.

They reached the field where they'd been digging that day. Father led them past the dark silhouettes of the beehive ruckles, the towers of drying turves; past the long winrows, the low piles. Frank looked down into the head where they'd dug out the black earlier that day. He saw the winrow he'd turned that afternoon, hot in the sun. His arms had ached with it, lifting the heavy wet turves. He couldn't believe water was that heavy.

'Keep up.'

He ran to catch up with Iris.

'Listen.'

Frank stopped. The crickets in the dry grass. A bird.

'A nightjar,' Iris whispered. 'You know about them?'

'Course I do,' Frank said.

'What do you know?'

'I know they go out at night.'

'But you don't know what they do.'

'They fly.'

'They find cattle and suck milk from their teats.'

'Birds don't drink milk.'

'Nightjars do. And you can't kill them neither,' Iris said. 'Unless you use silver. You can use silver bullets, or a silver sword. But it has to be silver.'

'You dunno what you're talking about,' Frank said, looking round the dark fields.

'You don't know anything,' Iris said, starting to run.

'I do,' Frank shouted, and he ran after her.

The field was a perfect square of uncut grass, surrounded on all four sides by rhynes. No trees, nothing. Just grass and water. Father led them into the middle. He sat down and told Frank and Iris to sit by him, one each side. 'There,' he said, 'now lie on your backs.'

They all lay down. 'Close your eyes. Tight.'

The three of them lay in the long dry grass, eyes closed. The noise of the field built up. Crickets, a nightingale, another nightjar.

Father laughed. 'Nightjar's come to find the milk, then.'

'See,' Iris said.

It was black inside their eyes and they could hear Father filling his pipe, pressing threads of tobacco down into the bowl. They heard the match on sandpaper and smelled phosphorus, then the sweet tobacco.

'Close your eyes, you bugger,' Father said to Iris.

'Yours closed, Frank?' Iris asked.

'Yeh.'

'Shush now,' Father said. 'Bide quiet for a minute.'

They lay, unmoving.

'When it's quiet and still like this, that's when God comes and walks the earth.'

'He comes down here?' Iris asked.

'Shush,' Father said.

'Can God walk?'

'Shush and lay still.' Then, 'Open your eyes. Slowly. And look straight up.'

The black sky. The moon. The stars.

'People think it's just a few miles of flat land down here, but they don't know.'

The sky expanded as they looked.

'The stars up there tell you the stories of the moors and Glastonbury. They tell us where we live and who we are.'

Frank felt the dry grass under his hands, pulled at it.

'Reckon I'll start with the story that started it all off. Look up, follow my finger up to the bright star there.'

They looked up and found the brightest star.

'Follow down and you'll see underneath there's a cross.'

They saw the cross of stars in the sky.

And they listened to the story.

And Did Those Feet?

The wind ripples the surface of the water. Deep beneath, peat lies in uncut layers. Between the two, the drowned land, where flowers drift, tethered by stems.

A fish swims through the floodwater, the blades of grass touching its belly.

April. A month of green in this, the pleasant land.

A rowing boat makes its way from the estuary, along the river, then across floodwater and over fields. Early morning sun on the water. Silver light. Oars dipping in, pulling, lifting, dipping in. There is another sound, a rhythmical sound, coming closer, and the boat slows. The man lifts the oars, rests them in the rowlocks. Two swans fly overhead, their wings up and down together, slow and heavy in the thin air, their feathers lit by the sun; white against the iron grey sky behind.

The man and the boy watch the swans, watch the white of them.

The drips of water and the fading rhythm of the wings.

Water and the boat. Nothing else.

That is all there is.

The man dips the oars back in, pulls against the weight of the water, and the boat begins to move.

The boy sits watching his uncle row. Then looking around

him at the stretch of water, the tree branches breaking through the silver surface, he yawns.

His uncle sees the yawn. 'You all right?'

The boys nods. 'Are we nearly there?' he asks.

His uncle laughs. 'You bugger,' he says. 'You're always asking that.' He points out the hill beyond, across the moors, where Glastonbury lies. 'Dry land.'

Not too far away.

'There'll be a bed for you there.'

The boy thinks of beds: the straw bed he was born in, the straw mattress he still sleeps on back at home.

He thinks of his mother, who lay on the straw bed and gave life to him.

His mother, the maiden mother, the untouched mother, the pure mother.

Who smells of home and straw.

Pure.

But the boy doesn't want to think of home, or his mother, so tries to think of beds instead. Beds and sleep, and how human beings go to sleep when the darkness comes and rise with the light. He thinks of the birds that fly at night here in this green land: the owl, the nightjar, the nightingale.

And he thinks of bats.

'Yeh, there'll be a good comfy bed for you.'

He saw a bat once, a dead bat. He hadn't known they had faces like that, little mammal faces.

'And some food for you.'

The boy looks up. 'Have you ever seen a bat, Uncle?' he asks.

His uncle nods. 'Seen a few bats in my time.'

'You ever seen their faces?'

'Funny faces.'

'They got big ears,' the boy says. 'You know, for their size.'

'It's all that hearing they got to do. I mean you can't hear like that unless you got the equipment.'

'Yeh,' the boy says. 'I spose.'

'Not got a big brain, bats. Yet they can hear like that. Makes you wonder.'

The boy looks round. 'Yeh,' he says. 'It does.'

'Maybe that's why God made them,' his uncle says. 'You know, get you wondering. If we were all the same, we wouldn't wonder much.'

'If we all had bat ears.'

'Bat ears and small brains.'

'If we all had small brains,' the boy says, 'we wouldn't be able to wonder.'

'True.' His uncle smiles. 'You're not daft.'

'Do you think,' the boys asks, looking around him at this strange land, 'it's only people who can wonder?'

'Mmm,' the uncle says. 'Nice to think animals could wonder.' He continues to row, then he says, 'So, what do you reckon of it so far?'

'Lots of water,' the boy says. 'Lots of water and very green.'

'Well, it's the water helps with the green.'

'Different from home,' the boy says. That word again. Home.

'It's good for you,' the uncle says. 'Get out a bit, see the world.'

They leave the boat at the edge of the town. Rope it to a tree, take the oars from the rowlocks and place them across the wooden seats.

The uncle reaches into the boat and takes out the bag of silver that he's going to exchange for the tin. He and the boy walk through the town to the house where he has arranged to meet the men. There the uncle talks with them of tin and silver, and they shake on the deal and pour drinks. The boy is led to the kitchen where a woman gives him a plate of fish and bread, and he eats till he can eat no more. Then he is led out the back, to the stables, where he is shown a long manger filled with clean, gold straw. He climbs in, and his eyes close as his head touches the straw, which smells of his mother.

His mother, on the bed of straw, giving life.
    The baby, the infant, eyes closed and mouth searching.
    Starlight in the dark of the barn.
    Pure.

The uncle rows the boat back across the floods. They walk to the harbour and get on board the trading ship, laden with the tin he traded for his silver. The boy sleeps in his hammock at night and mends ropes by day. He takes a long piece of rope and ties one knot in it every seven days. He has tied many knots by the time he reaches the heat and the arid land.

'Well,' his mother, Mary, says after she has held him and taken a step back to see how he has grown, 'what did you think of it?'
    'Well,' the boy says, 'it was green and wet and a good place.'
    'Is that all?' she says.
    'It made me think. I'm not getting any younger. I need to get on.'
    'What will you do?' she asks. 'Will you be a carpenter like your dad or a tin trader like Uncle Joseph?'
    The boy thinks. 'I want to work with people.'
    'You're not going to follow your dad?'
    'No. I'm gonna follow my own path.'

The boy's mother pauses then, 'Well, you got spirit. I'll give you that.'

The boy grew into a man and ended up working with wood, like his father. While he worked – turning, sanding, sawing – he thought about how he'd told his mother he wanted to work with people. About how he'd follow his own path. About how he hadn't.

It was on his thirtieth birthday that he decided. Dropped his carpentry tools and took up his new life.

Miracles, preaching, washing feet.

All sorts.

It was this new life that got him into trouble: he started to get a following, started to cause a stir. The whispering and planning against him began and he knew his new life would end.

It all came to a head in Jerusalem, where the Passover meal was prepared for him and his twelve followers. They sat at the table with the man's uncle, Joseph, and the man ripped a piece of bread off the loaf.

'Uncle,' he said, and held the piece of bread out to Joseph. 'Uncle who took me as a child and showed me the world. This is my body.'

Joseph took the bread. He ate.

The man filled Joseph's silver bowl with red wine. 'And this,' he said, 'shall be my blood.'

Uncle Joseph placed some of the bread in the silver bowl and it swelled with the wine.

'My blood and flesh,' his nephew said. He looked at the twelve men. Stood up. 'It's time to go. Our last supper together has ended.'

Joseph concealed the silver bowl under his robes. He stood and followed.

*

Jesus dragged his wooden cross for miles through the night, to the Place of the Skulls. At dawn the soldiers stripped him naked. They placed a purple cape on his body, a crown on his head, the thorns so thick they cut into his skin and the blood ran. Call yourself a king, they said, and spat in his eyes. Call yourself a king, they said, and beat him round the head with a reed cane, forcing the thorns deeper into his flesh. Call yourself a king, they said, and pulled out the hairs from his head and chin until more blood ran.

They nailed him onto the cross and raised it high, between two other crosses, between two thieves.

The wind blew and the birds fell silent.

Joseph stood beneath the cross, the silver bowl under his robes. He watched his nephew's lips move, watched him pray so hard that the sweat on his body became red and was blood. The drops of blood ran down him, down the cross, and sank into the dust. Fed the grasses.

Jesus' mother, Mary, stood with her hands over her eyes. Joseph placed his arm across her shoulders, then they turned from the scene. Left to prepare for the burial.

The heat on his skin. The dryness of his mouth. His arms. Shoulders. Legs. Chest.

'Water.' He cried out, again and again. 'Water.'

The sky darkened and he saw a robin fly in front of him then disappear.

A few minutes later it returned. Approached his mouth and touched its beak to his lips. A single drop of water fell into his mouth.

'Thank you,' he said.

The bird landed on his shoulder, its small claw feet digging into his skin. It cocked its head sideways, looked down at its breast. It was red. Wet blood.

'Thank you,' the man said again.

The bird flew off, returned, landed on his shoulder again. Its breast wet with blood.

'You want more?' the bird said. He nodded and the bird fed more drops of liquid into his mouth. He swallowed.

A bird, talking to him. He looked down at the earth. His chest, ripping open. His mind, it must be going.

'More again?'

He adjusted his arms. His weight dragged them down.

A bird, talking to him.

'I said, you want more?'

He shook his head.

'Right, well I'd better get off. Lot on at the minute.' The bird looked down at its breast. 'You know, I quite like this red, suits me. Could start something here.'

The man closed his eyes.

'Well, good luck,' the bird said. 'Spec they'll let you down soon.' It took one last look around, then flew off.

He could hear his own breathing. The sky darkened.

Water. He thought of cups, bowls of water. Streams, rivers, lakes, seas. Then he thought of the stretches of water he'd seen with his uncle. The sea, then the estuary, the river, the flooded land. He thought of leaning over one side of the boat and dipping his fingers in, bringing a cupped handful to his lips and drinking. He thought of lowering his face, lower and lower, until his skin touched the surface, until his whole head entered, then his neck and shoulders. His body slipping into the cool. Swimming. Down among the grasses. Down away from the light above, down deep, into the dark.

The sky darkened, black. The earth shook and ruptured. Saints rose from their graves and walked.

A soldier pierced his side with a silver sword. The uncle returned and took the silver bowl from under his robe and held it to catch his nephew's blood and water which mixed with the bread and wine. Flesh and blood.

When the body was cut down, it was given to Joseph. He took it to the tomb he had carved in the rock, wrapped it in a hundredweight of myrrh and aloes, then bound it in linen. He placed a boulder over the entrance to the tomb and left.

It was dark in the cave, even for the dead. A small crack of light where the boulder rested against the stone entrance. A noise there, a fluttering.

The robin flew in. 'They cut you down, then.'

His heart moved slowly, forced one drop of blood into a vein.

'See, I said they'd cut you down.'

One lung spread and grew and air ran through it.

'I met another robin after I saw you up there. She liked the red. It's still on me, you know.'

The other lung too. The heart slow but regular. Beating.

'Yeh, she quite liked it.'

He opened one eyelid. Saw the bird.

'That's better,' the robin said.

He opened his mouth. His lips. Dry.

'Now the other eye.'

He opened the other eye.

The robin hopped around. 'I reckon you're gonna be all right.'

The man moved.

'Here, let me give you a hand.' The robin found the end of the linen and pulled it with its beak, pulling and hopping along the floor until the linen strips lay in a heap and the man lay on the dusty floor, his skin coated in the leaves and sap.

'You'll need a clean-up,' the robin said, 'but you'll survive.'

'Thank you.'

'Christ,' the robin said. 'You can talk too.'

'I should say that to you.'

The bird laughed.

The man put his hand out. The robin hopped up onto it, stared at the man's palm. 'What's that?'

'What?'

The bird nodded its head at the mark on his palm. 'That.'

'Where the nails went in.'

'Christ.'

The man laughed. 'Can I stand up, do you think?'

The robin hopped down. 'Have a go.'

The man got slowly to his knees, then stood. He brushed the dust and dirt from his body and walked towards the light.

'Where you going?' the bird asked.

'See my uncle.'

'Well,' the robin said. 'Good luck.'

As the man pushed the boulder, the crack got larger and he started climbing through the gap. 'Thanks.'

'My pleasure,' the bird said.

The man turned back and looked at the robin. He smiled. 'Just one thing,' he said.

'Go on.'

'Have you always been able to talk to people?'

The robin shook his head. It looked puzzled. 'Hadn't thought of it, but no. Not till I saw you on that cross.'

'Right,' the man said. 'Well, I got to go.'

'Course.' The robin flew up to his shoulder. 'I'll see you.'

'Yeh. See you.'

The robin flew off and the man watched it go.

*

His mother embraced him and took him to see his uncle, who sat by the fire, head bowed.

'Uncle Joseph.'

Joseph looked up. His nephew standing in front of him, a small linen loincloth, skin stained green and brown. 'Christ alive.'

He laughed. 'Yep. That's right.' He sat by his uncle, by the fire. 'I've come to tell you something.'

'Tell me.'

'I want you to go and build a building. Where people can meet. Where the word can be spread.'

'Where?' his uncle asked.

'Sleep tonight and when you wake the answer will be there.'

Joseph lay that night by the fire with the silver bowl beside him. He thought of where he might build. Where he might hide the bowl so that no one would ever find it.

He finally slept for a few hours and woke at dawn to the sound of birds. Woke at dawn to the answer.

The wind on the water. Ripples. Silver light. Drowned fields. The uncut peat deep beneath the weight of the translucent floods. Flowers floating in the water. A fish below, grass brushing its belly.

Two swans in the light. The water and the two of them in the boat with the oars. Nothing else. Silence and stillness.

Joseph of Arimathea left that same day. He took followers and the silver bowl. They left the hot land and returned to the green. To the wet land.

∾

They lay still. On their backs in the long dry grass. In the night. Under the stars. Father refilled his pipe. He lit it and smoked.

Frank looked at the stars, at the cross they formed. The silence went on and on.

Eventually Iris asked, 'Are there more stories?'

'Yeh,' Father said. 'There's more.'

Silence again, then Frank felt for Father's hand, clutched at some grass with the other. Pulled it. Dry strands in his hand.

'We better get back,' Father said. But no one moved. They lay there in the dark, just the crickets and the birds, the sweet air and the night sky. Frank near to Father, Iris lying away from them, flat on her back, hair mixed in with the grass, her skin pale in the dark light, staring up into the night. The three of them with their thoughts.

Light Peat

When he woke it was dark still, just the small light on; someone sittting on the chair.

'That you, Brian?'

'Yeh. It's me.'

They were silent for a while, then Brian coughed. 'Margaret sent me up.'

'What time is it?' Frank asked. 'Must be getting on.'

Brian looked at his watch. 'Near seven.'

'Thought it was the middle of the night,' Frank said. 'Thought I'd dropped off for hours.'

'You want me to move the clock in here? I can do that if you like.'

'Don't want to know the time.'

'Right,' Brian said. 'There anything else I can get you?'

Frank shook his head.

Silence again, then, 'You managed all right while I was gone?'

'No problems,' Brian said. 'Mind, haven't been able to do a lot, what with the floods and that.'

'No.'

'You're all wired up, then.' Brian pointed at the drip.

'Bloody doctors,' Frank said.

'Don't want to be going to them in the first place, that's what I reckon.'

'Make work for themselves,' Frank said. 'Sending people for tests all the time. Soon as you're sat still, they get a needle in you, draw the blood out.'

'Well, you're home now.'

'Yeh. So you ain't been working?'

Brian stood. He pulled his jeans up under his belly. Sat down. 'Saw to Ivor's cattle.'

'George told me. In the boat.'

'Yeh. Cows go next month.'

'All of them?'

'He's had enough.' Brian stood up again and adjusted his belt where it was digging in. 'That's the way it's been going.'

'No one does any work down here now.'

'You wouldn't want to go back, mind. Not to working like you did.'

'You can't go back,' Frank said. 'So what's he gonna do, Ivor, when he's not got to milk?'

'Reckons he's gonna watch telly and drink.'

'Waste of good land.'

'You wouldn't say that if you saw it now. Most of it's underwater.'

'Always was a good bit of land.'

'Yeh, well. It's the way it's going.'

Brian scratched his chin and rubbed his sideburns. A pause, then, 'So. How you feeling, anyway?'

'Bloody marvellous.'

'Are you?'

'Don't be soft. How d'you think I am?'

Brian looked down at the floor.

Frank shook his head. 'Why's Ivor wanna go and do that? Give up like that?'

'He's not making the money any more.'

'It ain't right.'

'No. Well.' Brian rubbed his nose. 'George was good,' he said, 'while you were gone.'

'Yeh?'

'Yeh. We did a few jigsaws. Got that one done you gave him for Christmas. That one with the kittens. Heads were all right, but all that long fur, all the same colour. Tabbies would've been easier.'

'What else?'

'Took him out in the boat, like he told you. Made a few cakes.'

'Spec he missed me,' Frank said.

'Course he did, but we had a good time, mind.'

'Difficult for other people, you know, to know what's best for him, what he wants.'

'Maybe,' Brian said. 'Well, we managed anyway.'

'See, I know what he likes.'

'Yeh.' Brian moved and the chair creaked.

'You'll break that chair.'

'These jeans are getting tight, and they're new buggers.'

'Nothing to do with what you eat?'

Brian smiled. 'Course not.'

Frank stared at the window, the dark panes of glass.

'So it's better being back home, is it?'

'Yeh,' Frank said. 'Couldn't stand it there.'

'No. Don't reckon I'd like it much.' Brian rested his hand on his leg, drummed his fingers on the tight denim. 'I was sat here for a while while you were sleeping,' he said. 'You know, sat here thinking and that. And I thought, I wonder what they put in that.' He nodded towards the drip.

'Cider,' Frank said.

Brian grinned. 'Effect's the same, is it?'

'Similar.'

'Only ask cos it gets you talking.'

'What do you mean?' Frank said.

'You know, you been muttering this and that, shouted out a few times.'

Frank smoothed the covers. Coughed. 'Have I?'

'Yeh.'

'Well,' Frank said. 'Probably a load of old rubbish.'

'Yeh. Spec so.'

'Yeh. Load of nonsense.'

The sound of feet on the stairs and the door opened. George's face, looking in.

'Well, well,' Brian said, 'look who it is.'

'Who?' George asked.

'You, George.'

'Oh,' George said. 'I been watching the telly.'

'What was on?'

'Summat funny.' George came in the room and looked at Frank in the bed. 'I like summat funny on the telly.'

'Well, you like a laugh,' Brian said.

'Yeh. I like a laugh.'

'Where's Margaret?'

'Downstairs. She said you're to go and help her.'

'I spec she did,' Brian said. 'Help, help. That's all I do, George. It's a hard life.'

'We finished that jigsaw.'

'We did.'

'That was hard work.'

'It was.'

Brian stood up and pulled his jeans up where they were slipping again. 'Christ,' he said, 'they won't fit round my belly, so I put them under it and they fall down.'

'C'I sit on the chair?'

'Course you can. You sit there with your old dad.'

George sat down.

'You all right, Frank?' Brian asked. 'You all right if I go down?'

'I'm all right.'

'Right.' Brian clapped George on the shoulder. 'Good lad, George.'

'I'm a good lad.'

Brian left the room.

George, and Frank.

'I thought you were gonna get up,' George said. 'You know, for your tea.'

Frank lifted his hand, dangled the drip in the air. 'Bit difficult with this, Georgie.'

'Right.' George hummed for a moment, then trailed off. 'We had a big tea,' he said. 'Margaret cooked me chops and we had peas and chips.'

'That's good.'

'And we had my cake for pudding. With some custard Margaret made.'

'You like a nice custard.'

'A nice yellow custard.'

'Did you eat it all?'

'Yeh.' George clicked his fingers, then stood up, walked to the window and back. 'I wanna know when you're getting up.'

'When I feel well enough.'

'Ain't you well enough now?'

Frank shook his head.

'You been ill for ages.'

'I know, George.'

George shrugged. 'It's just. I don't like you being ill. No. I don't like it.'

'I know.'

George walked over to the wall. There was a crack in the plaster.

'What you doing?' Frank asked.

George didn't answer. He picked at the crack, widening it. Tiny pieces of plaster fell down onto the floor.

'George. What you doing?'

'Looking.'

'What for?'

'What might be in there.'

'There's nothing in there, George. It's just a crack in the plaster.'

Frank saw George's shoulders shrug.

'George.'

He turned round.

'It'll all be all right, Georgie.'

George nodded.

'Come and sit down.'

George walked back and sat on the chair. He rubbed his chin: the sound of bristles.

'That's it. You sit there and keep me company. I need a bit of company.'

'Maybe you could tell me a story.'

'I'm a bit tired for stories.'

They sat for a while, George looking at his hands, threading his fingers through each other, trying to turn them the other way up, to see the people in the church.

Here's the church, here's the steeple. Here are all the little people. He could remember the words but his hands wouldn't do it.

'George.'

He looked up.

'Is it raining? I can hear it.'

George tipped his head to one side, an ear cocked towards the window. 'I can hear something.'

'You open the window for me?'

George nodded, stood up and walked over to the window. The four equal panes of glass, the curled handle.

'Push the frame,' Frank said. 'Hard.'

As George pushed, the wood gave way and the window swung open. The rain sounded louder, falling steadily: slow, solid drops.

Frank could see the rain, silver in the light from the window. The wet tree outside. 'I can see the tree, Georgie.'

'It's raining,' George said.

'That's right.'

'Rain's water coming out the sky.'

'It is.'

George shook his head. 'Funny, water coming out the sky like that.'

Frank leaned back against the pillow and closed his eyes. The leaves on the tree moved in his mind, the rain falling onto them, the weight of the drops of water bending and twisting their green.

He opened his eyes. It was February. No leaves, no green, just dark wet branches and small silver buds.

He felt along the edge of the bed, found the drip then ran his hand down the length of the tube until his fingers touched the button.

'Dad,' George said.

Frank pressed.

'Dad, I been thinking about rain.'

It rushed through him, silver.

~

Frank watched his mother as she poured boiling water into the pot, then put the kettle back on the trivet by the range. Watched as she poked the fire, breaking up the turves and levelling them so they would burn out quicker. At the back of her neck some loose hair had fallen down and stuck to her wet skin, a darker red than the rest.

Frank took one of the slices of bread and put it on his plate, pulled the butter plate towards him and slid his knife in. The butter was soft, a deep yellow pool of liquid around it; it sank into his bread.

Mother turned to smile at him and he smiled back. She moved her big belly past the corner of the table and sat down, pushed the hair off her face.

'This heat,' she said. 'Gets right inside you.'

'Father said he'd take us to market today.'

'And the baby. Makes me feel heavy.'

'Can we go?'

She looked at Frank. 'Where?'

'Market. With Father.'

She shrugged. 'If you want to in this heat.' She took a piece of bread and placed it on her plate, then sighed.

'What will the baby eat?' Frank asked.

Mother smiled. 'Just milk for a bit till it needs more.' She poured milk into three cups and then the tea.

'Do all babies drink milk?'

'All of them.'

'Do birds drink milk?'

'Baby birds?'

'All birds.'

'They don't get it from their mothers. Not birds. Why d'you ask?'

'Nothing. What's in milk?'

She shrugged. 'Everything, I spose. Where's your sister?'

'Upstairs.'

40

Mother stood up and walked to the foot of the stairs. Called Iris's name.

Frank finished his bread, took another slice. While he buttered it and cut it into four equal shapes, Mother picked up her cup of tea and went outside, stood in the back doorway to get some air.

Iris came down the stairs and sat down.

'We're going to market,' Frank said.

'I know.' Iris held her tea with both hands and looked at the window. 'I didn't sleep,' she said quietly. 'Cos of the story.'

'It's just a story.'

Iris turned to him. 'I kept thinking of his hands. You know, when they put the nails in.'

'Then don't think about it.'

'Can't help it,' Iris said. 'Must've taken him ages to die, pinned up there like that in the sun. Imagine how his arms must have ached. And no water, and his dry mouth.'

Frank bit into one of the pieces of bread and butter.

'I'm gonna tell the baby when it comes,' Iris said. 'I'll take it out at night and show it the stars and tell it the stories.'

'It won't understand. Not straight away. Not till it's bigger.'

'It'll understand.'

'It'll be drinking milk. That's what they do.'

'I know that's what they do. I've seen a picture.'

'What picture?'

'At school. In that book about it all. That woman with the baby in the straw. Imagine that, having a baby in a manger cos there ain't no bed.' Iris drank. 'She was feeding it in the picture. You know, giving it her milk.'

Frank finished his bread and drank his tea. Iris sat in silence.

Mother came back into the room and refilled her cup.

'Did you hear us last night?' Iris asked.

Mother smiled. 'I didn't hear nothing.'

'You didn't hear Father going out?'

'No.'

'He took us out to see the stars,' Iris said.

'He start on his stories?'

Iris nodded. 'He told us the story about the man on the cross.'

'Is it true?' Frank asked.

'Course it's true,' Iris said. 'He's the baby in the straw.'

'*Is* it true?' Frank asked Mother.

Mother smiled. 'You better hurry up if you're going.'

Frank left the table, pulled his boots on, and went outside to wait for Father. Iris ate her bread quickly and followed.

They left the market and walked towards the moors, turning into a side road and climbing over a gate into the fair field. The sun behind them, on their backs and their necks. The three of them walked through the field and started to climb Wearyall Hill, a long, low slope where cattle grazed between the scrubby trees.

At the top they sat on the dry grass and rested. Iris pulled at the front of her dress and blew down it, but her breath was as hot as the air. Flies settled on the flanks of the cattle and sweat trickled down the back of Frank's legs. There were white dots in his eyes from the light and heat.

Father wiped his face. 'You all right?' he said to Frank.

Frank nodded.

'We'll stay here a minute.'

Iris lay down, then turned onto her side and looked at Father. 'The stories are true, aren't they?'

Father brushed a fly from his arm. 'Course they're true.'

'You're gonna tell us the rest?' Frank asked.

Father smiled. 'Look,' he said, nodding at the view. Glastonbury Tor at the head of the town, the Mendip Hills beyond. The flat moors running out to the sea.

'Where's home?' Frank asked, and Father pointed to the centre of the moors.

'You can't imagine it not hot like this,' Iris said.

Father smiled. 'It's the same place that flooded last winter.'

'I like the floods,' Frank said. 'Going in the boat and that.'

'Yeh,' Iris said. 'And no school.'

Father wiped his face again. 'This winter, there'll be the baby.'

They thought for a second, then Frank asked Father, 'Can the baby come in the boat if the floods come?'

'Course it can.'

'It can come in the boat and we'll tell it the stories,' Iris said.

Hail Hail

The hail rattled onto the boats and the surface of the water. Joseph, in the first boat, pulled his robe round his body, but the wind found its way through the cloth and cut into his skin.

The group rowed towards Glastonbury, across the floods, then along the river, till they reached the edge of dry land. They pulled the boats up onto the grass, took the oars from the rowlocks.

Joseph stood on the green grass where he had stood with his nephew all those years ago. In his hands he held a wooden box which he placed on the grass. Kneeling in front of it, he opened the lid and took out the silver bowl. The flesh and blood.

Silence for a long time.

Joseph placed the bowl back in the box and the men followed him to the foot of a long, low hill. He led the men up to the top, though they were cold and needed food and somewhere to lie down. They rested on the grass and looked at the view: the hills beyond; the town at the foot of the conical hill. And the flat, flooded land they had rowed across. Things they had never seen before: the greenness of the green; the stretch of water lying on the fields.

Joseph stood and raised the staff he had brought from the

dry land. 'Here,' he said, 'is the beginning.' He pushed the stick deep into the soft, wet earth. Named the hill Wearyall Hill.

The men walked into the town of Glastonbury and found a place to build the first building. They took long hazel sticks, shorn of leaves and twigs. They split them and bent them and wove them into panels. Built a frame for the roof. They dug holes in the earth and loosened rich soil, added chopped straw and water, mixed it into a thick paste to lay over the hurdles. They placed reed on the roof. Fixed it with split and twisted hazel sticks. A carpenter sawed and planed and made a table, the same shape as the table around which they had eaten the very last supper.

While the men built, Joseph spent his days walking the town and the surrounding hills. He looked over at the flat land and wondered where he could hide the silver bowl so no one else would ever find it.

Joseph's staff, meanwhile, remained at the top of Wearyall Hill. Surrounded by silence, earth and water, it began to take in the goodness of the soil. Tiny eyes on the stick, where the branches had been cut away to make it straight and smooth, started to swell and grow and fill with life. And the worn end of the stick that had tapped all the way from the dry land to the green sent its first pale root down into the dark earth below. It took in food and water and carried it to the buds above which split, putting out fresh tendrils. And the roots spread and the shoots grew and became branches which bore buds of their own. Then one day, the day of Jesus' birth, Christmas day, the buds burst into blossom.

*

The first year it blossomed, late in the day when the sky was dark and stars bright, Joseph climbed the hill to see it.

'A miracle,' he said. 'This is surely a holy thorn.'

He knelt by the tree and prayed, then opened his eyes, lay on his back in the grass and looked up at the sky. Looked up at the stars, at the shape of the cross. He thought of them all back at home, looking up to heaven, seeing the same pattern in their sky, then he closed his eyes and drifted away for a few minutes.

He woke, cold, his clothes damp from the grass. He opened his eyes and looked up at the sky. All those stars, still there. He stood up and was about to walk back into the town when he saw them.

They were in a circle around the Holy Thorn with its white blossom. In a circle and kneeling down.

A horse. A cow. A sheep. A goat. Two birds: one with a red breast, the other a magpie with no tail.

Joseph closed his eyes and opened them again. The animals still knelt.

He walked towards them.

Ran his hand down the horse's neck, felt the strong muscle beneath its mane. It was real. Warm, breathing. Horse. He lifted away his hand and stepped towards the goat.

'Do that again.'

He turned and stared.

'I said do that again. *Please.*'

In the dark of the night he could see its mouth move. The mouth of a horse.

'Was that you talking?'

'I've had sweet itch. You can't imagine what it's like, itching all the time.'

Joseph said nothing. Just stood and looked, at the tree grown from his staff, at the horse.

'You look surprised,' the horse said.

'I think I am. See, horses don't talk.'

'But I'm talking,' the horse said. 'So you're wrong.'

'I fell asleep.'

'But you're awake now.'

'I fell asleep on the grass.'

'This isn't a dream,' the horse said, 'if that's what you're thinking. This is life.'

Joseph stood still for a long time.

'We thought that's why you'd come here.'

'What do you mean?' Joseph asked.

'The hour after midnight, you know.'

Joseph thought for a second. 'No. I don't know.'

The horse looked at the cow. The cow shook its heavy head slowly.

'The hour after midnight,' the horse said carefully, 'on the day Jesus was born, we come here and in that hour we can talk to human beings.'

The cow nodded. 'We can.'

The robin stood up and hopped over to Joseph. It opened its beak. 'How do we know how long an hour is?'

The cow shook its head again. 'Come, come,' it said. 'Think, bird. The hour will be gone when you can't talk to humans like this one.'

'Ah,' the robin said. It flew up to Joseph's shoulder. 'Has this come as a surprise?' it asked.

'A surprise?' Joseph said. 'Yes, you could say that.'

'No one told you?' the horse asked.

'No.'

The robin reached out and touched Joseph's beard with its beak. 'That'd make nice nesting material.'

'You're not having it,' Joseph said.

'All right. Keep your hair on. I'm only saying.'

47

Joseph brushed roughly at the robin and it rose up into the air, flew around, then settled back on his shoulder.

'No need for that,' the cow said. 'Just a small bird. That's all.'

The horse turned to Joseph. 'He gets to me too. He's one of those.'

'I'm one of those what?' the robin asked.

'Never quiet. Always on about this and that.'

'Charming,' the robin said.

'What I don't understand,' Joseph said, 'is if you can talk . . .'

'Yes?' the cow said.

'Well, if you can talk, shouldn't we learn something from what you're saying?'

Silence. Then, 'Ah,' the cow said slowly. 'I think I see what you mean.'

The horse walked in a circle. It turned its head right round and bared its teeth, attempted to scratch its mane, but couldn't reach. Its long yellow teeth crashed together and it turned back to look at Joseph. 'You're trying to say something about what we're saying?'

'Well, I thought, you know, we may find something out.'

'Like?'

'Well, you know. Something.'

'He's taken against me.' The robin hopped along Joseph's shoulder. 'You have, haven't you?'

Joseph shook his head. 'Of course I haven't.'

'You think I'm stupid. Shallow.'

'Did I say that?' Joseph asked.

'Look, robin, leave the man alone,' the cow said.

'Leave us all alone, robin,' the horse said.

'That's the last time I give you a good scratch,' the robin said. 'What do you say, magpie?'

The magpie stood up from where it was kneeling and

48

joined them. 'I don't know what it is you think you should learn, but I have an idea about *why* we can talk to you.'

'There we are,' the horse said. 'Some sense.'

The magpie flew up and stood at the top of the horse's head, between its ears. 'You came from another land,' it said.

'I did.'

'And you came here for a reason.'

Joseph smiled. 'I did.'

The magpie nodded. 'You came to tell us about the other land. About someone you know.'

The goat trotted over to the group. 'That kneeling lark,' he said. 'I've had enough.'

'Ssshhh,' the cow said. 'The man's telling us something.'

'I mean how long do they expect us to kneel?' the goat asked. 'They're sore, my knees, and kneeling's the one thing goats do well.'

'You think you have a problem?' the robin said. 'Try it with these knees. Look at them.' The robin lifted one small brown leg. 'Can't even call it a knee.'

'Please,' the cow said. 'I want to hear what he has to say.'

'Hang on,' the horse said. 'Imagine the weight on my knees. The pressure.'

'Stop.' Joseph's voice was louder than he had intended. The word took a while to settle in the night air.

'Blimey,' the robin said. 'Was there any need for that?'

Joseph turned and saw the robin perched on his shoulder. 'I'm sorry.'

The robin moved its small brown wings up in a shrug. 'S'all right.'

'It's just – I want to tell you something,' Joseph said. 'About where I come from and why I'm here.'

'Go on,' the cow said. 'We're listening.'

'See, I came here years ago. With my nephew.'

'The foot-washer,' the robin said.

Joseph was silent for a second. 'How do you know?'

'You'd be amazed what we all know.' It looked round at the other animals. 'True?'

The cow nodded. 'True.'

'Word gets around, see,' the robin said.

'You know what happened to him?'

The magpie nodded. 'The miracles.'

'The foot-washing,' the horse said.

'And the terrible thing they did to him,' the robin said.

'Yeh,' the horse said. 'On that cross.'

'Poor man.' The cow shook its head.

'Course, I'd know about the stuff on the cross.' The robin puffed out the feathers on its chest. 'What with that starting the red breast thing.'

'And him coming back to life,' the goat said.

'With the help of a small bird.'

'Ah, but it was a goat supplied the milk to build him up a bit. After he'd died, he wasn't too well.'

'You wouldn't be,' the horse said.

'No. I don't spose you would,' the goat said.

'I have a question.'

'Go on,' Joseph said to the magpie.

'You know this miracle thing?' The magpie looked round behind it to where its tail had once been. 'Any chance of one being done now?'

'Ah,' Joseph said.

'I mean, he came back to life, didn't he?'

'He did.' Joseph nodded. 'He came to me.'

'So could he do something about my tail? It makes life hard for a bird, not having a tail.'

'Trouble is,' Joseph said, 'he's gone again.'

'Dead again?' the robin asked.

'Sort of. He will come back one day, though.'

'So can't you get hold of him?' asked the magpie.

'Not really. That's why I came here, you see. We've built a place on the edge of the town, where people can come and pray and listen to his teachings.'

'I saw you doing that.' The robin turned in a circle.

'And me,' the magpie said. 'I passed over a couple of times.'

The cow nodded slowly. 'They said you did a good job.'

'My knees still hurt,' the goat said.

'Shut up moaning.' The horse looked at Joseph. 'The birds were watching it all.'

'Watching what?' Joseph asked.

The robin moved closer to Joseph's ear and lowered its voice. 'You had something to hide.'

Joseph turned and looked at it.

'Something silver, they say,' the magpie said. 'I'm partial to a bit of silver myself.'

'Do you know where I put it?' Joseph asked the robin.

'Might do.'

'Tell me.' The magpie flapped its wings. 'Come on. You know what I'm like about silver.'

Joseph took a deep breath. 'Come on, robin. Tell me. Do you know?'

The robin flew down onto the grass. Hopped about, in circles. 'I'm thinking.'

'Come on, come on.'

A pause. Then the robin opened its beak.

Nothing.

'What is it?' Joseph said. 'Come on, tell me. Do you know where it is?'

The robin opened its beak again and nothing came out. It tried again. Nothing.

'What is it?' Joseph asked.

51

The cow lowered its head and moved it, from side to side. It opened its mouth, but all that came out was a rough pink tongue and a line of drool.

The horse shook its head up and down and the goat turned in a circle.

'Come on,' Joseph said. 'Talk to me.'

The cow opened its mouth again. Licked its lips with the pink tongue. Stretched its neck out. 'Moooo.'

The horse opened his mouth. Bared its teeth. 'Neigh.' Shook its head again.

The robin opened its beak. 'Peep.'

The magpie. 'Caww.'

And the goat looked up at the sky and the stars and let out a cry. 'Neeeeh.'

≈

The sun on the hill. The view over the flat land, out to sea.

Iris lay on her belly on the grass. Head on two hands, looking out over it all. She turned and looked sideways at Father.

'Where'd he hide it?'

'You'll have to come here at midnight this Christmas and ask the animals.'

'Does it really happen?' Frank asked.

'What d'you reckon?'

Frank thought for a while. 'I reckon so.'

Father smiled at him. 'You'll have to come and find out.'

Frank pulled his knees up to his chest. Wrapped his arms round his legs.

'You really want to know where he hid it?' Father asked.

Frank nodded. 'Yeh.'

'Course we do,' Iris said.

'Right. I better show you then.'

They walked down the hill, into the edge of the town. Followed the road towards the Tor until they reached a short path. At the end Father opened a gate and walked up to where a small stream emerged: water ran over rust-red stones, then sank into the earth. The Chalice Well.

'This is where Joseph came,' Father said. 'He put the silver bowl right down inside the well, so no one'd ever be able to get it out.'

'Why's the water red?' Iris asked.

'From the blood in the chalice.' Father dipped his hand in the cool water. 'The people who drank it found they were cured of everything. Breathing problems, blindness, deafness, the king's evil.'

'Can I try some?' Iris asked.

'Course you can.'

Iris cupped her hands in the water.

'Before you drink,' Father said, 'spill a few drops on the ground, for good manners.'

Iris spilled the drops which sank into the hot stones. She lifted some to her mouth and sipped. 'It tastes of metal.'

Father nodded. 'That's the blood.'

Iris cupped another handful and splashed it round the back of her neck, wetting her dark hair and the cotton of her dress, which stuck to her skin.

'You have some, Frank,' she said.

Frank shook his head.

'Go on. Might cure you.'

Frank looked up and Father smiled at him. 'Go on.'

'I don't need curing.'

'Course you don't. Just have a drink,' Father said.

Frank knelt down and cupped the water. He spilled some on the ground, then lifted the rest to his mouth. Spat it out.

Father laughed. 'It's holy water, Frank. From the blood well.'

Frank wiped his mouth with his arm. 'I don't like it.' He stood up.

Iris knelt back down, cupped more of the water, wet her face and the rest of her hair with it. She stood up. The water ran down onto her dress.

'Right,' Father said, 'time to get on.'

He started back towards the flat land and the two children followed.

Frank lay on the grass by his mother and watched Father hoeing, the blade swinging quickly, his body moving with it, the angle of the handle steady. The cut weeds fell.

Frank could smell his mother in the heat. Dark stains under each arm, a sheen on her face. As she leant back on her elbows, her dress stretched taut over her belly. The smell of her with the grass and the earth. Summer. Mother's hands were on the grass, her fingers red from work, black lines under her nails. A blue vein crawled over the back of one hand. Frank yawned.

Mother stroked his hair. 'Sleepy?'

Frank shook his head.

'It's the heat,' she said. 'Airless.'

Frank closed his eyes. The sound of the hoe again, slicing. The first cricket of the evening. And the smell of summer still, the grass and earth.

'He fallen asleep?' Father asked.

'Reckon.'

Frank half opened his eyes. The sun on his lashes, tiny circles of light. He tried to see the circles and the green of the grass at the same time, but couldn't.

'Too hot to cook,' Mother said.

Father nodded. 'I'll light a fire out here.'

'That'd be good.' Mother looked down at Frank, saw his eyes half open and took his hand. Placed it flat on her belly and he felt a movement, a leg drawing across. The limb under the skin, alive. He pulled his hand back startled, and Mother laughed.

Iris came out of the house, one hand over her eyes to shield them from the low sun. She walked over and sat on the grass.

The three of them sat in silence while Father hoed the end of the patch. Mother placed her own hand on her belly and laughed. 'Iris,' she said. 'Feel this.'

Iris shook her head.

'Come on.'

'No.'

'What was I like when I was a baby?' Frank asked.

'You cried and slept. Like Iris. Like babies do.'

'And drank milk,' Frank said.

'And drank milk.'

'How long will it be?' Frank asked.

Mother shrugged. 'How long it takes.'

It was getting dark, and the fire was still burning. Hot, red embers.

Mother yawned. 'I'm tired. Reckon I'll go on in.'

'We'll be in soon,' Father said.

Mother got to her knees and slowly stood up. They watched her walk to the back door and disappear, saw the lamp being lit and the flame move through the room, past the back window, until a few seconds later it appeared in the small window on the curved stairs, then again in the bedroom.

Frank looked up and saw the first stars. Father picked up a

stick, held it in the embers till the end caught fire, then passed it to Frank.

'Was Jesus the first one to come here?' Iris asked.

'No,' Father said. 'There were already people down here.'

Iris got her own stick, put it in the fire.

'How do they know?'

'From the peat,' Father said.

Iris took her stick out too soon; the end was black with a small red glow. She put it back.

'When you dig up the peat, there's stuff in there. Bowls. Tools. They found whole tracks where people walked across the wet land.'

'Who lived here?' Iris's stick was burning now and she waved it, watched the flames draw shapes of light.

'Hunters. People.' Father said. 'There was a lot to eat down here. Boars, pelicans.'

'They eat them?' Frank asked.

'Stuff like that, yeh.' Father put two more turves on the fire. 'The summer people, they called them.' Flames licked the edges of the turves. 'They used to come down in the summers when it was drier. They built a village in the end, on stilts with paths through the marsh.'

'Strange place to live,' Iris said.

'You live here.' Frank brushed his still-burning stick along the top of the grass, singed the blades.

'But it was all watery then,' Iris said. 'Even in summer.'

'People'll go where the food is,' Father said.

'They ever find any bodies?' Iris asked.

'Soil's too acid,' Father said. 'Would've eaten them away. Watch you don't set fire to everything, Franky.'

Frank held the stick so the flame ran along its length.

'Careful you don't burn your hand. They did find some stuff they reckoned was buried with bodies.'

'What would you be buried with?' Iris asked.

'My pipe,' Father said, 'and you two.'

'I'd be buried with a bottle of water and some food,' Iris said. 'In case I woke up and was hungry.'

'How you gonna wake up when you're dead?' Frank asked. 'Dead is dead.'

'You don't know what happens when you're dead.' Iris threw her stick into the fire.

'What about you, Frank?' Father asked.

Frank shrugged. 'Wouldn't like to be buried.'

The flame moved towards Frank's hand and he threw his stick in the fire.

They sat in silence with the sound of the fire.

The stars slowly coming out.

Frank opened his eyes in the morning, saw Iris kneeling in front of the open window, looking across the flat land. 'Iris.'

She continued to look, towards the hills beyond, towards Glastonbury.

'Iris.'

She turned round. 'What?'

'What you doing?'

Iris shrugged. 'I wanna go and see something.'

'What?'

She stood up. 'Get up and we'll go and see it. Then you'll know.'

The cottage was a simple building: blue lias stone walls with one door and two windows. A thatched roof. It was set in a small orchard, off the drove, and a dead pear tree was still pinned to the front, branches leading off either side.

Iris leaned on the gate, Frank next to her. 'What d'you reckon?' she asked.

'What am I sposed to reckon?'

Iris shrugged. 'You coming?'

'Maybe,' Frank said. 'If I want to.' He picked circles of lichen off the silvered wood.

Iris climbed the gate and started walking up through the old apple trees. He waited till she stopped and looked back, then put his foot on the lower rail, clambered over.

He pushed through the long grass, his feet flattening it, his fingers trailing over the seed heads. He caught up with Iris.

She picked one of the long grass stems. 'Here's a tree in summer,' she said, then pulled the seeds off, showed Frank the bare stem. 'Here's a tree in winter.' She held the small bunch of seed heads: 'Here's a bunch of flowers.' She threw them over Frank. 'And here's an April shower.' She walked off towards the house.

Frank brushed at the seeds, looked around at the trees and the cottage. He knelt down in the grass: the earth was hard under his knees. He lay down, on his back. Stared up through the grass at the blue above.

'Frank.'

A few leaves, a cluster of apples against the sky.

'Frank. Where are you?'

He turned onto his belly. That's what it'd be like to be an insect, crawling through the long grass, never seeing more than that.

'Frank, come on.'

He sat up. One of the grasses was barley, maybe dropped by a bird. They did that, birds. Carried seed to different places. It passed right through them. He picked the ear off the barley and it rattled with gold grains; he peeled back the coating and took out the tiny indented seed. Bit into it. Swallowed it. He ate another, then stood up and went to find Iris.

The door of the cottage was open. Frank pushed past it,

stepped over the fragments of glass on the stone floor. There was a cracked china sink and above that two shelves; the top one had fallen down at one end and rested on the bottom shelf. Two preserving jars balanced on the top shelf at an angle.

'Iris.' Frank went through the next door. An inglenook fireplace, the beam above cut from the trunk of a tree. The one window at the front. A tin bath against one wall.

'Iris,' he called again, pushing open the next door, into the last room. The roof had collapsed, and the thatch lay around the bare bedstead, caught on the wire base. There was clear blue sky above.

Iris stood at the window, looking out into the orchard.

'What you doing?' Frank asked.

'It's our house,' she said. 'We're gonna clear it up.'

Frank walked to the corner of the room. One boot lay on the floor, a small, child's boot with a worn leather sole. A walking stick leant against the cobwebbed wall. It had been whittled, the cuts deep into the bark.

Iris turned. 'Won't take long to get it right.' She rubbed the floor with her foot. 'Look, it's just earth.'

'I don't like it,' Frank said.

'Don't be soft.'

Frank picked a piece of plaster from the wall, threw it on the floor. 'I wanna go home.'

'You're too soft.' Iris ran her hand along the bedstead and rubbed the dust on her dress. 'You'll like it when we're done with it.'

'You don't know what I like,' Frank said.

'Do.'

'Go on then. What do I like?' Frank started to walk towards the door, but Iris pulled him back.

'You will like it if we do it,' she said. 'It'll be our house and no one'll know.'

'We got a house.'

'But we can come here and do things. We'll cook. You can light the fire.'

Frank thought for a second. 'You won't try and help?'

'I promise. You can do the fire.'

'So we'll need some turves.'

'That's it,' Iris said.

'And some wood from home. Get it going.'

'See, I said you'd like it.'

'I'll see if Father'll give me some stuff.'

'No,' Iris said quickly. Frank looked at her. 'You're not to tell.'

'Why?'

'Say it. Say you won't tell.'

Frank shrugged.

'Go on.'

'Okay. I won't tell.'

'Good.' Iris walked towards the door, then looked back at Frank. 'Good.'

~

The morphine was in his veins still.

Silver.

George on the chair still. And dark in the room still.

'You been asleep,' George said.

Frank closed his eyes again.

George waited.

'Did I tell you?' Frank said into the quiet of the room.

'What?'

'Did I tell you?'

George laced his fingers together and looked at them. 'Dad, I been thinking about fingers.'

'Yeh,' Frank said.

'They're clever, fingers are, when you think what they do.'

'George.'

'They do stuff without you even telling them.'

'George.'

'All sorts of stuff.'

'Did I tell you the stories?'

'What stories?'

'The foot-washer. The blood in the water.'

'I know them,' George said.

'I didn't tell you.'

'No. Margaret told me. Everyone knows them.'

'Yeh,' Frank said. 'Course they do.'

'This thing about fingers is, they're all different. The one in the middle's my biggest.'

'Has the rain stopped now?' Frank asked.

'Margaret says they all got different names. Peter Pointer this one is.' He held up his index finger.

'Has the rain stopped?'

'And there's Tom Thumb.'

Frank looked over at George, sitting with his thumb up, looking at it.

'He's not really a finger,' Frank said.

'Course he is. He's just a bit short and fat. That's all.'

'George.'

'I can't remember the others. I'll have to ask her again. It ain't easy all these things I have to remember.'

'No,' Frank said.

'Good job Margaret wrote down all the cake things. You know, how to make a cake.'

'Recipes.'

'Thought I'd make you a cake tomorrow. You can come downstairs and eat it with a nice cup of tea. That'd be good.' George smiled.

Frank looked away, at the window, open still. The rain falling still.

'Yeh,' George said, 'that'd be good.'

They sat in silence for a while, then Frank looked back at George. 'You were a good baby,' Frank said.

George smiled. 'A good baby.'

'The easiest baby anyone ever had.'

'I haven't got a baby,' George said.

'No.'

'Sometimes I think what it'd be like to have a baby.'

'And what do you think?'

'Well,' George said, 'it'd be nice sometimes. But what if it went on crying?'

Frank looked at the window.

'On and on. Crying. What would I do?'

Feet on the stairs.

'You were asleep before and you're awake now, Dad.'

'That's right,' Frank said.

The door opened. Margaret, in the doorway.

'So you must be feeling better,' George said.

'You all right, Dad?' Margaret asked.

Frank nodded, and George turned round to look at his sister. 'He's feeling better,' George said. 'He's coming down tomorrow to eat some cake.'

Margaret came into the room and stood behind George's chair, placed both hands on his shoulders.

'I don't think so, love.'

'He is. Only you'll have to make the tea, Margaret,' George said. 'I don't trust that kettle. Not when it gets hot like that.'

Margaret opened her mouth to speak, then closed it. She patted George's shoulders and took her hands away. 'You dropped off,' she said to Frank.

Frank nodded. 'A bit.'

'I popped in, see you were all right.'

'I just get a bit tired still. You know.'

Margaret nodded. 'You will. Only to be expected.'

'He had a sleep,' George said.

'That's right.' Margaret nodded again.

'You close your eyes when you sleep.'

'You do,' Margaret said.

'You close your eyes and the pictures come.'

'That's right.' Margaret moved round and sat on the edge of the bed. 'You were talking when I popped in, Dad,' she said. 'Kept saying things over and over. Iris, you said. Iris. Over and over.'

Frank looked at the window. 'C'you shut the window for me?' he asked quickly. 'I wanted to hear the rain, but it's a bit cold.'

Margaret stood and walked to the window, pulled it closed and turned the handle down. 'Yeh,' she said. 'You kept saying it over and over. Iris, iris.'

'Probably clearing rhynes in my sleep,' Frank said. 'Clearing out the irises.'

Margaret sat back on the edge of the bed. 'Spec you've cleared out a few in your time, eh?'

'A few,' Frank said.

'Irises are flowers,' George said.

'That's right,' Margaret said. 'You picked some for Mum when you were little, George. With me. Yellow, they are.'

George tipped his head to one side. 'Did I?'

Margaret nodded. 'Yeh. You did. Didn't he, Dad?'

Frank looked over at the chest of drawers, the white china knobs. 'Don't remember that.'

'I don't remember either,' George said.

'You can't remember everything,' Margaret said. 'Your brain has to get rid of things or it'd have no room, George.'

'Is everything in your brain somewhere?' George asked.

'Somewhere,' Margaret said. She turned to Frank. 'Can I get you anything, Dad? Tea or something?'

Silence for a few seconds.

'Doesn't the heat ever get to you?' Frank asked. 'In the summer when it gets still and hot and there's no air.'

'I dunno that I can remember what it's like. Can you, George?'

'I can't remember everything,' George said.

'Why d'you ask, Dad, when it's like this with the rain and that?'

'I dunno,' Frank said. 'Just fell to thinking, I spose.'

'You tell Dad what you did with Brian when he was away, George?'

'In the boat?'

'No. That thing you made. You know, that you hadn't done before. The thing with apples.'

'Oh,' George said, 'that thing.'

'Not an apple jigsaw?' Frank asked.

George laughed and clapped his hands. 'No.'

'Tell him,' Margaret said.

'Brian made this thing with me.'

'An apple cake?' Frank asked.

'Like an apple cake, only the apple was underneath all spread out, and the cake went on top. When it was cooked we turned it the other way and guess what?'

'You ate it.'

'We ate it, but before we ate it the apple was all on the top.'

'Yeh,' Margaret said to Frank. 'Brian did it with him. He was really good with him, Dad. Has so much patience.'

Frank looked over at the chest of drawers again. Looked back at George.

Margaret smiled.

'He's getting fat, your Brian,' Frank said.

'No harm in a bit of a covering in the winter,' Margaret said.

'He ought to be out working.'

'Where?'

'Get soft staying in all the time. There's plenty of jobs.'

'Ivor let him go, there's nothing else.'

'Plenty of work.'

'It's February, Dad.'

'Must be other work.'

'If he goes into town every day, but you know what he's like. I can't see him in town.' Margaret shook her head. 'Anyway, he's had George a lot while I been in and out of hospital every day.'

'Well, you didn't need to come and see me all that much. There wasn't no need.'

Margaret stood up. 'Well, thanks.'

'Bloody stupid me being there anyway. I mean what did they do? I was all right here.'

Margaret took a deep breath. 'How can you say you were? You weren't. You know that.' She walked to the door.

'And another thing,' Frank said, 'I don't need that doctor or nurse.'

'No. You said.'

Margaret left the room, slammed the door.

George looked down at the floor, then counted the fingers on each hand a few times. 'I don't remember that,' he said eventually.

'What?'

'Picking those irises for my mother.'

'No.'

'I think she died.'

'She did, George, a long time ago.'

'I don't think I remember her.'

'No.'

'So Margaret's right,' George said. 'You can't be remembering everything.'

Best Black

Frank looked at the peat turf in his hands. Wet black. Best black. He could see the fragments of earth and leaves. Part of a twig.

He started building a small hyle the way Father had taught him, placing the first turves on the grass. One row down, then two smaller rows to the sides. A crucifix. He propped up the other turves, leaving spaces so the air could get through to dry them out. It was odd how heavy the turves were when wet. Odd how heavy water was. Odd that something so wet could end up being burned on a fire.

'Franky.'

He looked up. Father was lining out the new head with his spade. Other men were there; women too, in white aprons. The grass and topsoil were being put into the old head, exposing a flat black surface ready to cut.

'Come here, Franky.'

He walked over.

'You all right?'

'Hot.'

Father nodded. 'Let's go and get a drink.'

They made their way to the edge of the field, to the rhyne, and sat in the shade of a willow. Father undid some string tied to the tree and pulled. The duckweed on the surface of the rhyne moved, a china flagon emerging, covered in the green. Father leant forward and looped his finger through the hole in the handle, pulling it up onto the grass next to them. He uncorked it and offered it to Frank.

Frank drank the cider and passed it back. Father drank and then they sat in silence, the sun on their skin, the smell of cider, and the sound of the spades behind them down into the peat, their blades cutting into the layers.

Father lay back, one hand on the flagon, and closed his eyes.

Frank watched a small fly land on his arm. He brushed it away and it moved, only to land again on his hand. There were spots of green weed on Frank's fingers, from the flagon. He tried to brush them off, but they stuck to his other hand. He wiped them on the grass.

Father sat up. 'When I came to help my dad once, we was sat like this and he told me to listen.'

Frank listened.

'Nothing?'

Frank shook his head.

'He told me the withies grew so fast on a hot day you could hear them.'

Frank looked up into the tree: the thick stump and the thin willow branches. 'I can't hear nothing.'

Father laughed. 'Since then I always reckon I can hear the plants growing. Hear their leaves rustling. Stems stretching.'

'Can you?'

Father shrugged. He drank again, passed the flagon to Frank. 'Reckon you can hear anything if you want to enough.'

'I'd like to hear things.'

'What would you like to hear?'

Frank lay down. 'That story again,' he said. 'The animals talking.'

Father laughed. 'Thought you liked that one.'

Frank turned onto his stomach and picked a blade of grass. 'There's more stories still, you know.'

Frank watched a woman putting the last turves on the cart, watched the horse take the weight and the cart move forward. 'Who told you them?'

'Everyone knows them.'

The cart left the field and started up the drove towards Glastonbury.

Father pushed the cork in and leant forward, dropping the flagon into the rhyne. They watched it disappear, watched the duckweed close over the space where it had sunk. Father tied the string to the tree again. 'We better get on. Come on.' He stood up, took Frank's hand and pulled him up. They stood in the sun, and Father held Frank's hand for a second before letting go.

Late evening and deep light in the room. The smell of the pipe. The window: four squares of glass and the curved handle, open. Warm air inside and out.

Frank looked down at his leg where it hung out of the bed. The brown skin. The dirt round his ankle. The bare wooden floor beneath.

Sounds outside: birds and Father's low voice.

Too early for sleep; too hot for sleep.

Frank swung his leg and watched it move across the boards. He looked at the door, at the half-floorboard underneath it. Floorboards ran across from the window to the bed; Father had taken one up to see how bad the worm was. He'd shown Frank the joists, running the other way. That's what you nailed boards into, the joists.

Frank yawned. He turned and lay on his back. He could just make out the crack in the white plaster. It ran across one

71

corner and each day it was what he wanted it to be. The coast, where land met sea. The edge of a hill. The path of a river. Things could be anything you wanted them to be. If you wanted hard enough.

Feet on the stairs and Father and Iris came in. Frank closed his eyes.

'Come on,' Father whispered. 'You need a good sleep.'

They walked across the room and Frank heard Iris's clothes fall to the floor. He opened his eyes, saw Father there.

'Still awake, Frank?'

'Bit.'

'Come on, Iris. In you get.'

Iris got into the bed and Frank felt her, hot against his side.

Father sat on the end of the bed. 'That better?'

Iris nodded.

'Good. You not tired, Frank?'

'Not yet.'

'Ought to be. You worked like a man today.'

'I worked too,' Iris said quietly.

'You should've seen him, Iris. All day building hyles, he was.'

'Dad,' Iris said.

He looked down at her.

'You know what I did today?'

'Christ, look at you. Cover yourself up, girl.'

Iris pulled the covers up to her neck.

'You wanna be wearing summat in bed. Girl your age.'

Iris shrugged.

'Will you do one of the stories?' Frank asked.

'You got to get some sleep.'

'Oh, go on,' Frank said. 'Please.'

'You're a soft pair.' Father leant back against the bedstead.

Merlin's Coffin

Joseph of Arimathea has been dead for a long time, sleeping his long sleep in the green land. The small wooden church has gone: the daub has dissolved in the rain and seeped back into the ground. The thatch has fallen in and been carried away by birds for their nests. The hazel wattles have unravelled and been burned on fires. Only the table has survived. It is in the courthouse in the town, and men sit behind it and pass judgement.

Down in the earth, below the level of the sea, water runs unseen, carving a path through the bedrock of blue lias stone. In this water sits the Holy Grail. Unfound. Leaking blood.

'What we need,' King Arthur said, 'is a table.'

'A table?' Merlin said. 'Why would we need a table?'

'Why do you think we need a table?'

'To eat around? To hide under?' Merlin took out his big sword and cut off the chicken's head. He threw the naked, headless chicken onto the pile on the grass.

Arthur brushed brown feathers from the front of his armour. He turned his chicken over and carried on plucking.

'I don't see,' Merlin said, 'why we need a table.'

Arthur rubbed his cheek and left a small feather there, stuck to his skin with blood. 'You know, I thought you were wise.'

'I am wise.'

'We need a table for the Knights to sit around and plan.'

'Ah. For planning.'

'We'll sit around it and plan everything we do next.'

Merlin shook his head. 'And do you want to say what kind of table we may need?'

'Something big enough for all of us to fit around.'

'Anything else?'

Arthur pulled out the last of the feathers and handed the chicken to Merlin, who cut its head off, added it to the pile.

'Not just a table table,' Arthur said.

'I see. And are you going to explain what a table table is?'

Arthur picked up another chicken. 'How many of these do we need, exactly?'

'Exactly the number that are by your feet,' Merlin said. 'Or I wouldn't have wrung their necks.'

Arthur held up the chicken's floppy neck and looked it in the cloudy eye. 'Bet you wish you hadn't gone off lay now.'

He answered himself in the chicken's voice, shaking its head as it spoke. 'I should have pushed those eggs out day after day.'

Arthur again, 'Well, you'll make a lovely stew.'

'Oh,' the chicken clucked. 'I'm in a right stew.'

'You will be,' Arthur said. He looked at Merlin and grinned.

'Have you finished?' Merlin asked.

'I think so.' He put the chicken down.

'So we need a table table?' Merlin said. 'You going to tell me what that is, seeing as I have to find you one?'

'A table with a past.'

'Go on.'

'A table of substance.' Arthur shook his head. 'Do you know, this is quite putting me off the thought of eating them.'

'A table of substance?' Merlin asked. 'You mean heavy?'

'Don't you start. You know what I mean.'

'Substance,' Merlin said.

'Yeh. Substance. A table with a history, with some meaning. Oh, and enough room for all of us to fit around.'

'You said that already.'

'Well, it's important.'

'And shape?' Merlin asked. 'Any special requirements? I spose you're going to say dodecahedron.'

'I hadn't planned to.'

Merlin laughed. 'You wouldn't. You don't know what it is.'

'Do.'

'Don't.'

Arthur stood up. 'I've had enough.'

'Go on,' Merlin said. 'What is it, then? Tell me.'

Arthur kicked the chicken and its body thumped into the plucked corpses. 'Stupid birds.'

'Dodecahedron. Come on, think it through.'

'I said stop it. Just go and get me a table.'

Merlin shrugged. 'If that's what you want. Any old shape, then?'

'Why would I care about the shape of a table?' Arthur took the sword from Merlin's side. 'I'm off.'

'And who's going to do the chickens?'

'Not me. I'm a king, you see.'

'Yes,' Merlin said. 'I had noticed.'

Arthur wiped the blood from the sword, put it into the scabbard he wore on his belt and walked away.

Merlin shrugged and picked up another chicken. He took a handful of feathers and was about to pull, when he thought: a table of substance. A table with some history.

He knew the very table.

*

The men sat around the table and ruled the land. For years there was peace, until the most pure and noble of the Knights came to the table and described a vision he had seen: a quest. The Holy Grail, the vessel containing Christ's blood, which Christ's own lips had touched at the Last Supper, was to be found and returned to the dry and holy land.

Arthur thought about this for a while. He closed his eyes and held his fingers together, thinking.

Merlin tapped him on the shoulder. 'A word.'

Arthur brushed him away, clapped his hands together. 'From now on,' he said, 'we shall dedicate ourselves to finding the Holy Grail.' He stood up.

'Please, a word,' Merlin said.

'Noble men,' Arthur continued, 'Knights of the table, we shall search the length and breadth of this land until we find this object.'

'I beg you,' Merlin said. 'One little word. It'll save a lot of work.'

'Enough,' Arthur shouted at Merlin. 'Horses, we need horses.'

Years passed, Arthur and his Knights galloping on tired horses, out of the town of Glastonbury, by the foot of the Tor, passing the end of the path that led to the well where the red water flowed night and day.

With the Knights away, Merlin was left to look after things. He was rubbing beeswax into the table to make the grain glow when Arthur's illegitimate son, Mordred, arrived.

'Ah, Merlin,' he said. 'Arthur sent me to see you.'

Merlin put down his cloth and closed the wooden box containing the beeswax.

'He sent me with a message, that he lies dying, and that

he wishes me to take over the table. He wishes me to marry Guinevere when he dies.'

Merlin nodded slowly. 'Anything else?'

'Like?' Mordred asked.

Merlin held one hand up. He pointed to the first finger. 'You want his kingdom.' He held up the second finger. 'You want his wife. Presumably you want his home?'

Mordred shrugged. 'I hadn't thought that far.'

'Well, let's chuck the home in anyway.' He held up his third finger. 'What about his armour? He has a spare set here with his spare horse.' He held up the fourth finger.

'Look,' Mordred said. 'You're making this complicated. It's simple.'

Merlin shook his head. 'Nothing is simple. Never has been. In fact the whole concept of simplicity is flawed.'

Mordred stamped one foot. His chain mail jangled. 'Shut up. Just shut up.'

Mordred sat at the table and spread out his hands. It was a good table. He liked it.

Merlin entered and bowed. 'Some news I thought you should hear.'

'You may have overdone the wax,' Mordred said. 'It's a bit sticky to the touch.'

'Your father,' Merlin said, 'who you say was dying, has been seen coming close with his army of men.'

Mordred looked up. 'Ah. It seems my father's made a good recovery, then. A miracle, perhaps.'

Mordred gathered his men and lay in wait in the flat fields surrounding Glastonbury. Arthur and his men neared, then hid in the grass and rhynes. Silence from both sides and the light fading.

One of Arthur's men was dropping off to sleep when he saw it. A yellow and brown flash and the arrowhead pattern on its skin. The adder reared up, its tight body on end and its fangs wide open. The Knight drew his sword and cut off its head.

The sun, the last of the day's light, flashed on the silver blade, giving the signal for the battle to begin.

For this is often how a battle begins. An error. A small movement.

Mordred pierced his father's head with his sword and King Arthur, bloodied and confused, was taken back towards Glastonbury. As he crossed the river Brue, he hurled his own sword, Excalibur, into the water. He died before he reached the town.

They buried him in a hollowed oak tree deep under the ground, within an hour's slow walk of the Holy Grail. Later, when Guinevere died, she too was placed in the same oak tree. There they lie, even now, waiting to rise up to save England.

Merlin was the only one left and he took to walking around the town. Took to sleeping in the porch of the church, in a pile of rags. When winter came he moved into the church. People from the town tried to move him, told him he couldn't stay there, but every evening he bedded down and every morning he woke.

The man who kept the shop next to the church brought him a hot drink one time. Merlin sat up in his pile of rags and held the drink in his filthy hands. He sipped.

'Now look,' the man said, 'it's not good for you, living like this. Not good for you or for the town. You're not getting any younger, Merlin.'

'Not getting any older, either,' Merlin said.

The man smiled. 'We need to sort something out, we can't go on like this. We'll find you dead here one morning.'

Merlin finished the drink and laughed. 'No hope of that.'

'You never know. Sleeping rough like this.'

'Ah,' Merlin said. 'But I do know. Everlasting life, I have. I shall be here in this churchyard after you've all died.'

'Oh. I see.'

Merlin shrugged. 'Only thing that can kill me is gold.'

'Gold, eh?' The man thought for a second. 'Listen, you fancy another drink?'

The man gathered the people from the town and they sat around the table.

'You got to think of trade,' the man said. 'Think of what it does to the town to have him there. It's only him now, but before you know it the High Street'll be full of them.'

The people nodded.

'We need a plan,' the man said.

While Merlin slept in the church, the people of the town brought their gold, any gold they could find, and took it to the farrier, who melted it in vast pots and poured it into a mould. He made the sides, the base and the lid. A gold coffin.

During the night, the men from the town took the coffin onto the moors. They hid it deep in a dry rhyne and laid grasses, bulrushes and irises on top of it.

The following morning the man took Merlin his hot drink.

'You're a good friend,' Merlin said. 'A real friend.'

'Mmmm,' the man said. 'Merlin?'

Merlin looked up from his drink.

'We been thinking. A few of us said it's been a long time since you saw anything other than this church.'

'True.'

'So we thought we'd like to take you out today.'

Merlin finished the drink and stood up. 'That's good of you,' he said. 'A change of scene'll do me good.'

It was at the edge of town that they jumped him. Pulled him to the ground and strapped him to a hurdle, which they carried over the moors until they reached the rhyne. There they untied him and pushed him into the pile of grass, bulrushes and irises.

'You can't drown me.' Merlin laughed at the men, but then he saw the gold lid coming down onto him, and he screamed.

The lid was closed and he lay inside the gold coffin, in his bed of grass and flowers.

~

A silence in the room. The dying light and the warm air.

'They buried him alive,' Iris said.

'Yeh.'

Silence again.

'Is he still in there?' Frank asked.

Father shrugged. 'Probably.'

'And no one's found the coffin?' Iris asked.

'They've looked.'

'Maybe we could find it,' Iris said. 'If we look hard enough.'

Father laughed. 'Lot of land to search.'

'Poor man,' Frank said.

'The monks found King Arthur's grave,' Father said. 'In the abbey.' He got off the bed and leant an arm on the bedstead. 'He still had the marks on his skull from where he'd been killed.' He dropped his voice slightly, moved towards them. 'There was another skeleton in with him, had long blonde hair. One of the monks touched it and it turned to gold dust.'

'Guinevere,' Iris said.

'That's what they say.' Father took his arm off the bedstead. 'Time for sleep,' he said.

Iris nodded.

Father walked to the door and opened it. 'And no talking.' He left and closed the door.

Frank leaned back against the trunk, his knees gripping the branch, the bark rough on the soft inside of his legs. He stared at the pattern of the leaves against the sky. The stars must be up there, waiting.

He looked over at the house.

'Frank.' She was there, by the door to the house. He could see her looking for him. 'Frank, where are you?' She walked through the grass, calling his name. He pulled an apple off the tree, small and sharp, threw it so it landed near her. She looked down, then up at the trees. 'You nearly got me.'

'I never.'

'What you doing?' she said. 'We got things to do in the house.'

Frank started to climb down.

'Come on,' she said. 'We got to make a start.'

He stood for a moment in the long grass, then followed her. They went through the kitchen into the main room, through into the bedroom. The open sky and the thatch on the bed and floor. The thick cobwebs around the stick. The one boot on the earth floor.

'I don't like this room,' Frank said.

'You scared?' Iris asked.

'Course I'm not. Don't be stupid.'

'You're being a baby.'

'Shut up.'

Iris picked up an armful of reed from the bed and carried it over to the wall under the window.

'What you doing?'

She gathered another armful, knelt down on the earth floor and started to shape the reed into a nest.

Frank scuffed his boot on the earth floor. Iris turned to look at him standing there, watching her.

'Tired, are you?' She spoke in Father's voice: 'Worked like a man.'

'Shut up.'

'All day building hyles, he was.'

Frank walked towards the door. 'I'm going back.'

Iris jumped up and grabbed his arm. 'Don't go.'

'I dunno what you're doing.'

'I'm just doing the house. That's all.'

'Do we have to do it all now?'

'Got to be done for the baby.'

'You won't be able to bring the baby. Not till it's big.'

Iris laughed. 'Not that baby.'

'What baby, then?'

Iris shook her head.

'What baby?'

'Nothing.' Iris let go of Frank's arm. 'We're gonna need a pan,' she said. 'For cooking. When you light the fire.'

'I'm getting hungry now.'

'Just stay while I do this. I'm nearly done.'

Frank shrugged.

Iris walked over to the nest of reed and carried on shaping it, Frank watching her.

When she'd finished, she turned round. 'How long d'you reckon it took him to die?'

'Who?'

'In the gold coffin. How long would he've been there?'

'Dunno,' Frank said. 'How long's it take to die?'

'Spose it depends what you die of.'

'What did he die of, then?'

Iris stared up at the hole in the roof. 'Must've stopped breathing.'

'Ten minutes?' Frank said. 'An hour?'

'Where d'you get that from?'

Frank shrugged. 'Spec that's how long it takes.'

Iris shook her head. 'I keep thinking of him, seeing that gold lid, then scratching at it, trying to get out.'

'Then stop thinking of it,' Frank said.

Iris laughed. 'Thinking isn't like that. See, things go on and on, round and round, and there's nothing you can do about it.'

'Maybe he died really quickly,' Frank said.

'No.' Iris looked back at the reed bed by the wall. 'No. I think it took a long time. Try and stop breathing. See how long you can do it for.' She took a breath and held it, till Frank could see her face starting to redden.

'That's long enough,' he said.

Iris shook her head.

'Stop it.'

She looked away, then let out a breath and laughed. 'Did you think I was gonna die?'

'Course I didn't.'

'You did. Thing about you, Frank, you don't understand things.'

'I do.'

Iris smiled. She reached behind and undid the top button of her dress. 'Will you look at something?' She let the dress slip off her shoulders. 'Look.' She turned around.

'What is it?' Frank asked.

'Look at my freckles.'

Frank looked closer.

'Look at the pattern of them,' Iris said. 'They're the same as the stars.'

'What you talking about?'

'The stars and the stories. They're all on me.'

'They're just freckles.'

Iris grabbed his shirt. 'They're the stars.'

Frank shook his head, took a step back. 'I got to get home. I'm hungry.'

Iris pulled her dress back over her shoulder. Did up the top button.

Frank left the room and Iris watched him walk through the orchard, down to the gate, then she ran after him.

~

Dark. The room was dark but it should be light. He was walking home along the drove. The sun on his skin. Iris following.

A hand on him, touching him. He pushed it away. 'I want to go home.'

'You are home.'

Wanting to go home. Wanting to be helped up the stairs. To lie down. In the room with the square window, with the whitewashed walls and the wooden floor.

'Dad.'

Wanting to sleep.

'Dad. It's me, Margaret. You're all right.'

'The sun's hot.'

'There's no sun. It's raining still.'

He tried to turn in the bed, but something stopped him. Pulled on his arm.

Rain. It was raining still. Floods. Layers of water over the peat, over the flat land. The stumps of willow trees, the gateposts. Silver water in the light.

'It's the morphine, Dad. That's what it is.'

Silver water in his veins, lapping. His blood the tide, in and out.

The moon and the stars and the tide.

He opened his eyes.

'Iris?'

'No, Dad. It's me. Margaret.'

'Margaret.'

'The morphine,' she said. 'It's bound to confuse you.'

Morphine. That's what it was.

'Oh, Dad.' Her voice was quiet. She took Frank's hand and he let her.

'I had a sister. Iris. Her name was Iris.'

Silence. Then, 'I didn't know.'

'I thought,' Frank whispered.

'What? What did you think?'

'I thought I'd forgotten.'

He closed his eyes and Margaret stayed there, his hand in hers. The rain outside the window. Night moving on.

'What time is it?'

'Half past nine.'

Frank nodded. 'It is today still?'

Margaret smiled. 'Yeh, it's today.'

'I mean the day I came home.'

Margaret stood up. 'You came home today.'

'Feels like I been here for weeks.'

'It would, I spec.' She smoothed the bedcovers. 'You need anything?'

'Bit of water, maybe.'

She picked up the glass and held it to his mouth. He swallowed. 'Where's George?'

'Downstairs watching telly with Brian. I told him to leave you alone for a bit.'

'Will he come up now?'

'If you want him to. Don't want him bothering you.'

'He's never bothered me.'

Margaret sat back down.

Frank closed his eyes and they were quiet for a while. Margaret swallowed, then opened her mouth to speak. 'Will you tell me about Iris?'

There was a long silence.

'You said, earlier,' Margaret said.

Another silence.

'I didn't know, you see.' She cleared her throat. 'Not before you told me.' She waited, but the silence continued. 'Right,' she said eventually. 'Well, I ought to get on.'

Frank struggled to move and Margaret jumped up. 'Here, let me help you.' She adjusted his pillows and helped him to sit up.

'That better?'

Frank nodded.

'So,' she said. A pause. 'I don't like winter.'

Nothing.

'Days are too short. And these floods. I told the doctor to come first thing. Brian's got to pick him up in the boat.'

'I told you. I don't need a doctor.'

'They have to come. You know, for the drip, or you'll run out.'

'Don't need anyone.'

'No. Well, what am I doing here then?'

'What are you doing?'

Margaret took a breath and waited. Then, 'Look, can I get you anything?'

'Nothing I need.'

'Right. Well, raining still.'

'Yeh.'

'Rained like this last year, you remember?'

'No.'

'All that sun in March and we knew we'd pay for it.'

Frank plucked at the corner of one of his pillows which had folded over and was digging in his neck. Margaret leant forward and straightened it. 'Twenty-two days of rain in a row. Something like that. I remember seeing it on the telly.'

'Your Brian watches too much telly.'

'He's all right.'

'That's how he's got that fat. Ain't right.'

'Why d'you say that?'

Frank looked away.

'For God's sake, Dad.'

'Well,' Frank said. 'All that fussing over George.'

Margaret ran her foot along the crack between the boards. 'We couldn't have managed without him.' Her voice was calm, quiet.

'On and on he goes. You should've had your own kids for him to fuss over.'

Margaret looked at him as he lay in the bed, staring straight ahead. His lips tight together.

'Don't you think that's what we wanted?'

Frank shrugged.

'You can't say that. You know you can't.'

'Say what I like. It's my house.'

'Dad, don't say that. You know you shouldn't.'

'Well, tell him not to fuss at George.'

'Right.' Margaret walked to the end of the bed and leant on the bedstead. Frank turned his face away. 'You want to talk about George? That's fine by me. You know he thinks you're getting up tomorrow.'

Frank shrugged.

'Well, you can't let him go thinking that. You know what he's like.' She shook her head.

Frank picked at the bedcover with his free hand. A tiny piece of the fabric came away in his fingers, a thread of cream cotton.

Margaret walked towards the door.

'Where are you going?'

She turned. 'To send your George up.'

'Reckon I could eat a little summat.'

'Well, I'll send something up with George.'

'There's no need to be like that.'

Margaret fiddled with the latch. 'Like what?'

'You know what.'

Margaret waited a second then, 'No, Dad, I don't know.'

She let the latch fall down. Closed the door and went downstairs.

George sat by the bed, a plate in his hand. He wore pyjamas and a thick dressing gown. His favourite shoes with bare feet. His ankles thin and white. Dark hairs.

'Got some sandwiches,' George said. 'Margaret cut the crusts off. She said your teeth weren't strong enough for crusts.'

'She did, did she?'

'Yeh, she did.'

'Break a bit off for me.'

George tore into the soft sandwich.

'What's in it?' Frank asked.

'Mashed-up egg. Good for you, she says.'

Frank nodded. 'I like an egg.'

George held out the piece of sandwich and Frank took it between his fingers, moved it towards his mouth but it fell before he could eat it.

'You dropped it,' George said.

'I know.'

'Pick it up, then.'

'You pick it up,' Frank said. 'Anyway, I'm not hungry now.'

George shrugged. He leant forward and picked up the piece of sandwich and put it in his own mouth. 'I been watching the telly. With Brian.'

'What you been watching?'

'Something with police in it. In a city. Lots of people in it.'

'Lots of people in cities.'

'Yeh,' George said through another mouthful. 'That's what Brian says. He says he went to Bristol once.'

'Yeh,' Frank said.

'You been to Bristol, Dad?'

Frank shook his head. 'Been to Taunton.'

'Have I been to Taunton?'

'With me. To the market.'

George thought about it, then nodded. He finished the sandwiches and put the plate on the table.

'Has the rain stopped?'

'Dunno.'

'Have a look for me.'

George stood up. He wiped his hands on his trousers. 'I liked that sandwich.' He walked towards the door.

'The window,' Frank said. 'You can look out of that.'

'Oh.' George pushed the swollen wood and opened it. 'Does it stop when it runs out of rain?'

'No,' Frank said. 'It stops when it stops. Then the sun comes out and it all goes back up in the sky.'

George stared at him.

'Maybe it is when it runs out. I don't know. So has it stopped now?'

'No.'

George left the window open and sat back down. Frank could see egg round his mouth. Crumbs on his new jumper.

George looked round the room. 'Walls've always been white in here.'

'That's right.'

'It was white when you were a boy.'

'It was.'

'Was I born in this room?'

'Yeh.'

'Were you?'

'No,' Frank said. 'I was born in your room.'

'But I was born in this room.'

Frank nodded. 'You were a lovely baby.'

'I wasn't no trouble.'

'You'd lay there for hours, just playing with your fingers.'

'Peter Pointer and his friends.'

'That's it.'

George smiled. 'I look a bit like my mother.'

'You do.'

'That's what everyone says.'

'You're the spit, George.'

'Yeh, I'm the spit.'

Frank shifted in the bed, adjusted his weight.

'Did your dad die of oldness?' George asked.

'Sort of. He died when you were young. His heart stopped one day.'

'Why?'

'Just did. Happens like that sometimes. Gets worn out, or it's all clogged up.'

'Will that happen to you?'

'No one knows what'll happen to them.'

'Does that make you go yellow?'

Frank shook his head. 'That's summat else. In the blood.'

'I don't like blood,' George said. 'No, I don't like blood.'

'Don't think anyone likes blood.'

'That story, the man on the cross.'

'The foot-washer.'

George smiled. 'That's the one. Full of blood, that story.'

'Some are.'

'Like people,' George said. 'People're full of blood.'

'That's a horrible thought.'

'You reckon I ought to close the window?'

'Maybe that'd be a good idea.'

'Right.' George patted his knees. Rocked his feet on toes then heels. 'Dad.'

Frank waited then, 'What?'

'Do I have to go to the centre tomorrow?'

'You ain't been all week, cos of the floods.'

'Oh,' George said.

'So you ain't going anywhere tomorrow.'

'So I'm staying here?'

Frank nodded. 'Yeh. You're staying here.'

George clapped. 'All day here with you.'

The bedroom door opened slowly. Brian came in and closed it behind him.

'All right?'

Frank nodded.

'You all right with him here?'

'We're fine, ain't we, George?'

'Yeh.'

Brian walked to the end of the bed. 'You all right if I prop myself here?'

'Long as you're not sat on my feet.'

Brian laughed. 'See the window's open.' He took a pouch from his pocket. 'Mind if I have a smoke?'

'Margaret'll get after you,' Frank said.

'She's dropped off.' Brian took out a paper and straightened it. Added the threads of tobacco and started rolling. Licked and sealed the paper. He lit the roll-up and George waved the smoke away. 'If those buggers of doctors could see, eh?' Brian said.

Frank laughed. 'Shame they can't.' He tried to move to a more comfortable position.

'You need help?' Brian asked.

Frank shook his head. 'I'm all right.'

'Want a puff?'

Frank shook his head.

Brian took another few drags, then threw the fag end out into the rain.

'They said when the rain's gonna stop?' Frank asked.

'More low pressure coming in.'

'You close the window? Getting a bit cold.' Frank moved his hand towards the button.

Brian noticed. 'You all right?'

Frank nodded. 'Bit cold. That's all.'

'Right.' Brian pulled the window closed and turned the curled handle. 'We better leave you in peace. Come on, George.'

'I'm staying here,' George said. He held onto the seat of the chair with both hands.

'You ain't. You're coming with me.'

George shook his head. 'I wanna stay with Dad.'

Frank held the button. Stroked it with his finger.

'Come on, your dad's tired. Needs some sleep.'

Frank pressed the button. The silver water.

'But it ain't night.'

'It is, near enough.' Brian took George's arm and pulled him gently out of the chair. The chair lifted from the floor too. 'We could make some cakes.'

'Now?'

Silver water and the boat moving slowly. Water dripping down.

'Yeh, now,' Brian said. 'But only if you come downstairs.'

'Right.' George let go of the chair and stood up.

'That's it, George. Good boy.'

'I'm a good boy,' George said.

'You are. You are a good boy.'

'I was a lovely baby. Never no trouble.'

'You're no trouble now.'

'No.' George looked back at Frank. 'Is he asleep?'

Brian turned. Frank's eyes closed and his hand on the button still. The smell of fags heavy in the room.

'Yeh, he's asleep.'

~

Iris and Mother sat at the back of the house where the shade fell down from the eaves. Mother leant back against the wall. Her legs apart. Her hands resting on her belly. Iris sat cross-legged, drawing in the dust with her finger.

'Never have a summer baby,' Mother said. 'You want a baby born in the spring.'

'Like me.'

'Like you, yeh.'

'I want a baby,' Iris said.

Mother laughed. 'You better wait a while.'

Iris drew a circle in the dust and another within that. She looked up at her mother's belly.

'Can you just have a baby?'

'You have to lie with someone.'

Iris thought for a moment. 'Not always.'

'Unless it's a miracle.'

'Miracles happen.'

'Maybe.' The baby moved under Mother's hand. 'Quick. Feel it,' Mother said.

Iris shook her head. She stared down at the dust.

'Go on, Iris. It'll be born soon enough.'

'Don't want to.'

Mother could feel the baby under her ribs, turning inside her, pushing against the bones. 'Here they are,' she said. Frank and Father walking back over the rhyne and towards the house.

Iris stood up. 'I'll get the tea on.' She walked to the well and drew up a fresh bucket of water. Took it into the house and left it in the sink. Went into the other room and moved the kettle onto the fire. Got the pot ready.

Frank came in. He took his shirt off in the scullery. Plunged both hands into the bucket of cold water and splashed it on his face and on the back of his neck. He put his shirt back on his wet skin and walked out.

Iris filled the pot and waited. Through the open window she could see the allotment and the hen house. A bee flew too close to the glass and caught a leg on the corner of a web. Iris watched it pull free and fly off, trailing a thread. She turned from the window and poured the tea into the cups, took them out on a wooden tray.

Father put his tea on the ground and went into the house to wash.

Frank sat in the shade beside Mother, Iris the other side. The three of them with their backs on the wall. The flagstones beneath them were the temperature of blood.

'Good girl,' Mother said. 'Couldn't get up if I tried.'

Frank ran his finger down the crack between two of the flagstones, teasing out tiny cubes of moss. A red spider mite ran over his finger and he squashed it on the stone. It left a red stain.

Mother dropped a hand down and slowly rubbed Frank's hair. 'Father said you're working well.'

Frank smiled.

Iris stood up. 'I'll get the cakes.'

Mother's hand still on his head in the heat. He watched Iris walk into the house.

'You tired, love?'

'I'm all right,' Frank said.

A chicken scratched at the ground, making a dirt bath. Black dust and the rustle of the feathers.

Iris came out carrying a wooden breadboard heaped with squares of cake. She passed one to Mother who took it and bit into it, the crumbs spilling down her dress. 'Is it good?'

Mother nodded.

'Frank?'

Frank took a square and ate it quickly. Iris gave him another.

'Hungry work, Frank,' Mother said.

'I worked hard too.'

'Course you did. You're a proper help.'

Father walked towards them. Water ran down his chest and darkened the top of his trousers. 'You made some cakes, Iris?' He bit into one.

'Is it good?'

'Not bad.' He picked up his tea and drank. Sat down on the flagstone next to Frank, reached over and took another cake. 'These got oatmeal in them?'

'Yeh,' Iris said.

'Thought they did.'

Frank looked up at the sky, dark afternoon blue. One blurred cloud beneath the sun.

They sat there. Too hot to move or talk. Father took a third square of cake and finished it. 'Makes you wonder.' He brushed his hands together to get rid of the crumbs. 'This bit of flat land and all those stories.'

'You're a soft bugger,' Mother said.

'I know that,' Father said. 'I know.'

A Softish Dough

The year 878. King Alfred, England's Darling, was in hiding from the Danes, who had ransacked his very green country. His fort was hidden deep in the Somerset flatlands, on a scrap of dry land, cut off by all but one causeway.

One morning he woke and looked out of his stone slit of a window.

'I have to get out,' he said.

'You can't do that,' his servant said as he poured warm water into a silver bowl for the king's morning wash. 'You're a king in hiding.' He started humming and the king placed his hands over his ears. 'Thing about a king in hiding,' the servant continued, 'is you have to hide.'

'Do I?' the king asked.

The servant headed for the door. 'Yes,' he said. 'You do.'

The king dressed in his plainest clothes and walked through the vast wooden doors. Outside, his guards stopped him.

'Let me pass,' he said.

The guards looked at each other.

'I am the king and I want to pass.'

One guard nodded at the other and they allowed him past. He walked up to the guards at the end of the causeway and they bowed and he passed.

The sun shone and made him happy. Heavy cow parsley filled the droves and he picked a flower and sniffed at it, tossed it in the air. He skipped, feeling heady at being outside with the feel of the sun on his skin. Oh, what a weight it is to be a king. What a weight.

Small birds swooped down and landed on the hedgerows.

The king climbed a gate and balanced on it, looking around. What a wet land this had been back in the winter. When the floods were bad and the rain never stopped; he'd been on an island. One man on an island.

It wouldn't be long now before he was ready to get his country back and build up what had been destroyed. Those Danes.

He walked further down the drove. The may blossom smelled heavy; he could see the flies dancing round it.

Those Danes.

He should have come out before, it was doing him good. It would help clear his thoughts. Nothing like a good, clear thought.

He heard a noise, brushed it away. A cow, or those birds rustling around.

He walked faster, though he was sure it was nothing.

The noise again.

King Alfred stopped and listened. Feet. He was sure he could hear feet. But it could be anyone. Could be his servant coming to check on him. Could be one of the guards.

Could be a Dane.

He looked back down the drove, but could see nothing. Just the grass and the fields.

The noise again, louder. He started to run.

He ran until he reached the cowherd's cottage that lay ahead. Ran straight through the open door. Closed the door behind him, leant back against it. Caught his breath.

It was quite dark inside. Small windows and thick thatch on the roof. It took time for his eyes to adjust from the bright sunshine outside.

'And who are you?'

A large woman, hands dipped in a bowl.

King Alfred looked at her and smiled.

There was one room beyond, with what looked like a pile of rags in a corner. And in here the fireplace, the table and the woman. Did people live like this?

'I said, who are you?'

He cleared his throat. 'Your husband?'

'Out with the cows.' The woman brushed her hair away from her face with a floury hand. 'Milking time, ain't it?'

'Ah,' the king said. 'Right.'

'You shut the door.'

The king nodded. 'I did.'

'Bit forward, I thought,' the woman said. 'Coming in here, no word of a hello.'

He nodded again. 'You're probably right.'

'So are you gonna open it?'

He shook his head. 'I don't think so.'

'No?'

He cleared his throat. 'Can I stay a minute?'

'Why would you want to do that?'

He shrugged. 'I just need to avoid someone. Someone I knew coming down the drove.'

The woman stared at him. 'Whatever,' she said, walking over to the shelves on the wall.

'Perhaps I could help you.'

She turned.

'You know, with whatever you're making.'

She shook her head. 'You're a funny bugger.'

'I've not done it before, but you could tell me what to do.'

'We'll give it a go,' she said. 'If you like.'

'Right.' The king rolled up his sleeves. 'What are we making?'

'Oatcakes.'

'Cakes. I love a cake.'

'Oatcakes. Like biscuits.'

'Ah,' he said. 'Right. Well, you just tell me what to do.'

'I've put the oatmeal in.'

The king looked in the bowl.

'Bit of salt.' The woman threw in a pinch.

'Shall I mix it?'

'You mix it.'

He mixed it with his bare hand. There was something black in the oatmeal and he picked it out. It moved.

'Weevils,' the woman said. She dropped it on the stone floor and stood on it. The crunch of its crisp body. 'They get everywhere.' She walked to the fire and got a small bowl of fat she'd melted. 'Pig fat.'

'In a cake?'

'*Oatcake*.'

'Right.'

She poured the fat into the bowl and the king continued mixing. The woman addded some water from the kettle.

'Hope it's not Danish pig fat.' The king laughed until he had to bend over. The woman stared at him. 'Just a little joke of mine,' he said, wiping tears away.

He mixed and the woman watched. 'Am I done yet?' He tipped the bowl towards her.

The woman sighed. 'You really haven't done this before. Keep going till it's a softish dough.'

'A softish dough.'

'That's it.' She put a flat black pan on the fire.

The king mixed and the dough became a softish lump.

The woman sprinkled oatmeal over the table and took the dough from the bowl, rolled it out and cut it into triangles.

'Not that difficult,' the king said. 'Reckon I could do some on my own next time.'

The woman ignored him. She placed the triangles on the hot plate. 'I'm gonna leave you here,' she said. 'You keep an eye on them. You have to turn them in a few minutes, when they're lightly browned.'

'Lightly browned.'

'That's it.'

'A softish dough and lightly browned.'

The woman nodded at him. 'Turn them in a few minutes, then take the pan from the heat and they'll be done.'

'Right.'

The woman walked to the door and opened it. 'Just don't burn them,' she said, and she left.

He stood over the black shapes on the hot pan. Looked at the open door into the garden. Looked at the bowl still on the table. Looked at the shelf. He walked over. Oatmeal? Where would he find oatmeal? Where would he find bacon fat?

'Still here, then?'

He turned and saw her in the doorway. Standing with a cabbage from her garden.

'Ah,' he said.

She frowned at the hot pan on the table. The black triangles.

'Are those my oatcakes?'

He picked one up. Bit the edge of it. 'They're not so bad,' he said.

She ran the two steps to the table. Picked up the pan and threw the oatcakes into the fire. Put the pan down and walked around the table towards King Alfred.

'Listen,' he said.

100

'No.'

'But you must.'

She picked up the rolling pin. 'No.'

'I need to tell you something,' he said.

She ran. Around the table.

He ran. 'I have to tell you,' he said, 'who I am.'

She caught his shoulder with the pin and he cried out. Ran towards the open door.

'Get out,' she screamed. 'Get out. Get out.'

And he did.

~

The wooden breadboard was bare.

'Did she find out he was a king?' Iris asked.

Father picked up some of the crumbs and put them in his mouth.

'They told her later. She made him some more oatcakes as a present and took them round to the guards.'

Mother pulled her dress tight over her belly.

'She really hit the king?' Frank asked.

'Yeh.' Father looked at Mother's belly. 'Look at you. You're ready to go.'

Mother laughed. 'Feels like it.'

Frank placed his hand on his mother's belly. It was hard and taut. 'It's not moving.'

'Too hot to move. It's sleeping, I spec.'

Frank smiled. 'Funny to think of it sleeping in there.'

'Yeh,' Mother looked at Iris. Reached out a hand to push her dark fringe off her forehead.

Iris pulled away, shook her off.

'You all right? You look tired.'

'I'm all right,' Iris said.

'All these late nights, Father's stories. You wanna get some sleep.' Mother leant her head against the wall and closed her eyes.

'I said I'm all right.'

'I like that story,' Frank said.

Father nodded. 'I thought you would.'

'Why are all the stories round here?'

Father smiled. 'That's just how it is.' He leant back against the wall and closed his eyes too.

Frank took his hand off his mother's belly.

Iris rubbed out the circles in the dust.

Frank watched the chicken get up from its dirt bath and shake all her feathers. Black dust. She folded her feathers down and walked off. Frank prised more cubes of moss from the flagstones. Piled them all in a heap and then started breaking them into smaller pieces.

Father made a noise in his throat. He opened his eyes. Adjusted his head. Went back to sleep.

The tops of the trees swayed in the lightest of winds, and the swallows moved in the blue, high up above where the four of them sat in the shade. High above where they sat on the blood-warm stones as the sun sank through the sky.

Fenwood Peat

Margaret looked at Frank, his eyes closed, one arm straight by his side, the tube appearing from under the bandage. The other arm crossed over his chest.

She gazed round the room. The white walls, the window. The chest of drawers. Nothing had changed since she used to come to see George in his cot.

She walked to the window, stared out into the night.

Behind her, Frank moved and Margaret turned around. His eyes were open. 'You're there, then.'

'Yeh, I'm here.' She sat beside him.

He lifted a finger and pointed at her. 'You won't find it there.'

'What won't I find?'

'See, it could be anywhere.'

Margaret waited, then, 'Course it could.'

'Moors stretch right over to the sea.'

'Right to the sea.'

'Yeh. That's it.'

Margaret waited, then, 'What am I looking for?'

Frank tried to sit up. Margaret put out a hand, tried to stop him.

'You know, Iris,' he said. 'You know what you're looking for.' He lay back against the pillow. 'See, you can't keep going to the house. Not with the baby coming. And autumn'll be here soon enough.'

'It's all right. I'll help,' Margaret said.

'Good. You're a good girl, see.' Frank closed his eyes.

Margaret watched him for a long time.

Eventually he opened his eyes again. 'George?'

'Downstairs,' Margaret said.

'He's never right. You know that.'

'I know that.'

Frank closed his eyes once more.

Margaret waited while he drifted off for a while. Then he spoke, 'Are you there?'

'I'm here.'

'Don't go.'

'I'm not going anywhere.' Margaret laid her hand gently over Frank's.

'There's things in my head.'

'I know.'

'All this in my head.'

'It's all right, Dad. You're all right.'

Frank opened his eyes. 'I don't know what's what any more.'

'You're here with me. I'll look after you.'

Frank tried to pull his hand away and Margaret let him.

'I said before, it's the medicine.'

Frank shook his head.

'You warm enough? You feel cold to me.'

'Bit.'

'Bet Brian had the window open. I can smell his fags, you know. He must think I'm daft.' Margaret looked over at the fireplace. 'What if I lit you a fire?'

Frank nodded.

Margaret stood up. 'I'll go and get some coal.'

Frank watched her go. He stared down at his hand. The bandage and the tube. Glanced over at the open door, the light on the landing. He closed his eyes and waited.

When Margaret returned, she carried a newspaper and a bucket of coal and kindling. 'We'll warm you up soon enough.' She knelt in front of the fireplace and screwed the paper into loose balls, placed it in the fireplace with the kindling. Picked out smaller lumps of coal and piled them high, then took matches from her cardigan pocket and struck one: the paper burned quickly and the wood caught.

Margaret sat back on her heels and watched the flames spread, until the paper was ash and the wood was burning. She added some more small lumps of coal; one fell out, rolling onto the hearth, and she put it back. Rubbed her hand on her jeans to get the black off. 'Nice to see it lit again.'

Frank nodded. 'Not the same as peat though.'

'No,' Margaret said.

'When I was young, I couldn't understand how peat could burn when it'd been so wet.'

'Did you help dig a lot?'

Frank nodded. 'Most days,' he said. 'We all did.'

'D'you miss a lot of school?'

'Didn't have much need of school.'

'No, I spose.'

'It was a long way to school. Not like jumping in a car now. We'd catch the train to Glastonbury. With the peat.'

'I know. Different world now,' Margaret said.

'Yeh. Nothing's left of that one.'

'But there's a new one now,' Margaret said.

'Not the same.' Frank shook his head. 'Sad that, when you see a whole world die.'

'Come on. Some things must be better now, eh?' Margaret

pushed one of the sticks of kindling into the centre of the fire. 'Well, that's taken.'

'Can't think of any.'

'You wouldn't be at home now.' She pointed at the drip.

'Wouldn't have known I was ill, wouldn't have had those tests.'

'Yeh, well,' Margaret said, a note of impatience in her voice.

'People used to die in their chairs by the fire. Bit of a cold on the chest. The old man's friend.'

Margaret stood up, her knees stiff from kneeling. 'I don't think it was that easy. Anyway, the world's how it is now.'

'Spose at least we got a proper fire.'

Margaret sat down. 'George is still up.'

'What's he doing?'

'He's been making cakes again.'

'Wasn't he tired?'

'I think he was too excited you're home. You know what he's like.'

Frank smiled. The flames lit the room, moving on the walls. 'What time is it, then?'

Margaret glanced at her wrist. 'Half eleven.'

'Going on forever, today. Half eleven, you say.'

'Just gone.'

'You may wanna get on to bed, eh?'

'No. We're all right.'

'Must be tired.'

'I dropped off downstairs.'

They listened to the fire. The flames burning and the coals shifting in the heat.

'Dad,' Margaret said.

Frank watched the flames.

'Dad. We're gonna have to talk about George.'

'Ain't nothing to say.'

Margaret waited.

'There ain't.'

'But what's gonna happen?'

'No one knows what's gonna happen.'

'Dad.'

'I don't want to talk about it.'

'You mean you don't want to think about it.'

'That's enough,' Frank said.

'If that's how you want it.'

'That is how I want it.'

'Fine.' Margaret stood up.

'Where you going?'

'Downstairs.'

'No need to be like that.'

A pause. Margaret gripped the back of the chair, took a deep breath. Looked down at the floor, then up again. 'You warmer now?'

Frank nodded. Closed his eyes.

'I'll go and check on them downstairs,' Margaret said. 'You look like you could do with some peace for a bit.' She smiled and waited, but Frank was silent. She left the room quietly.

The sound of the fire and the feel of the plastic tubing. Frank opened his eyes.

One night, George had been ill and slept in this bed. Frank had lit a fire and sat on the wooden chair. All night. The two of them. George on the bed, his pyjamas undone to the waist. The light from the fire on his white skin. The flames burning until dawn.

It'd been a long night.

Now the fire died down, the coals sinking and shifting in the flames.

*

There were feet on the stairs and the door opened. George, in his pyjamas. 'Dad.' He walked over to the bed, put his hand on Frank's shoulder and shook him. 'Dad, it's me, George.'

'The cakes ready?'

George laughed. 'They're cooling down.' He sat on the chair by the bed. 'Brian likes making cakes.'

'Who's Brian?'

George clapped his hands together and laughed again.

Frank looked at him. 'You got another story?'

'You want me to tell you a story?' George asked.

'I looked at the stars.'

'Course you did,' George said. 'You showed me the stars.'

'We lay in the grass and looked at the stars.'

'We did.'

'And Iris was there.'

'Iris?'

'Iris was with me.' Frank tried to sit up. 'Why's the fire lit?'

'Margaret said you was cold.'

'But this heat and the way it gets to you down here.'

'It's raining still.'

Frank shook his head. 'Ain't never been so hot.'

'Dad, what you talking about?'

Frank stared at George.

'Dad.'

'Who are you?'

There was a pause, then George said, 'Me.'

Frank shook his head. Closed his eyes and opened them again.

'I don't know who you are.'

George slapped his head with his hand. 'Stop it.'

'Sun's going down now.'

'It's not. It's night-time, Dad.'

Frank stared at him still.

'I'm George. George Francis Lovell.'

Frank continued to stare; George raised his thumb to his mouth and bit it, yelped and stood up. Went to the door and shouted for Margaret. When he turned back, Frank's eyes were closed.

Margaret ran up the stairs. Into the room. Put her finger to her lips. 'George, he's asleep.'

'He was talking.'

'I told you not to come in here.'

George bit his thumb again and stood up, paced across the room.

'What is it?'

George shook his head.

'Come on, George. It's all right. Sit down.' Margaret knelt in front of him and took his thumb out of his mouth and held his hand. 'It's all right,' she soothed. 'It's all right.'

George put his other hand to his mouth, but Margaret pulled it away and they stayed there for a while, George in the chair and Margaret kneeling in front of it. Holding his hands.

'Why did you call for me?'

George looked over her shoulder at Frank. 'He said he didn't know who I was.'

Margaret dropped George's hands, placed her own hands on his upper arms. 'Look at me. That's it. It's the medicine he's on, that's all. It confuses him. He doesn't know what he's saying.'

'Does it confuse you?'

Margaret smiled. 'I'm not taking his medicine.' She pointed at the drip. 'See, it goes up there. Goes straight in his arm, in his blood.'

'I don't like blood.'

'Sshh,' Margaret said. 'You got to whisper.'

'I can whisper.'

'Good.'

'He said he's hot,' George said. 'Shall I put the fire out?'

Margaret stood up. She walked up to Frank's head and placed her hand on his cheek, then felt the back of his neck. 'He's fine. He's not hot.'

George looked at her. 'I told him it wasn't hot. I told him it was raining.' His voice, rising.

'Shush. Whisper, remember. Aren't you tired yet?'

'Don't want to go to bed,' George said. 'Not with Dad home.'

'You'll need some sleep.'

George shook his head. 'Don't want to go to sleep.'

Margaret smiled. 'We all have to sleep.'

'Why?'

'To rest.'

'But I am resting. In the chair.'

'You get tired if you don't sleep. Animals sleep.'

'All of them? Even fish?'

'Yeh. They sleep. In the water.'

'And birds?'

'They stop in trees to sleep.' Margaret moved towards the window. She turned around. 'Except swifts. They can sleep in the air.'

George shook his head. 'You can't sleep in the air.'

'Well, swifts can.'

George thought for a second, then, 'Can animals talk?'

'Not to you, no. Maybe they talk to each other.'

George smiled. 'Maybe.'

'Now come on,' Margaret said. 'Time you got some sleep.'

George looked back at Frank. 'He needs me here.'

Margaret walked to George's side and touched his shoulder. 'He's all right.'

'He'd like me to stay all night.'

'Well, you can't, George.'

George frowned. 'Why?'

'Cos he'll sleep better on his own.'

'You reckon?'

'Yeh, I'm sure. He needs some quiet now, needs a good night's sleep. See, if we leave him, he may sleep all through the night.'

'Like a baby.'

'Yeh. Like a baby.'

'I used to sleep through the night.'

'You still do, George. You still do.'

George stood up and Margaret took his arm. 'Come on.'

He took two steps, then stopped. 'Do you remember my mother?'

'I do, yeh.'

'I don't remember her.'

'You were quite young.'

'And my memory's not very good. Dad said.'

'Well, no.'

'Did I like her?'

Margaret smiled. 'Course you did. She was your mum.'

'What happened to her?'

'She died, when you were little.'

'Summat in the blood.'

'That's right.'

'See, I remember that. I don't like blood.'

'No, you don't.'

'And Dad looked after me.'

'He did. I helped a bit too. Now come on, time for bed.'

George took one last look at Frank, asleep, still and silent against the pillow. 'All right,' he said. 'Time for bed.' As he turned to walk out of the room, a bubble of air was released from Frank's mouth and his lips curved into a smile.

'Maybe he's dreaming,' George said.

'Yeh, maybe he is. Come on.'

~

Upside down on the earth floor, the tin bath became a table. Frank stood at it, mixing oatmeal and water in a bowl, stirring it with a stick.

'It should have fat in.'

Iris glanced at him. 'I know that.' She shook her head. 'You better hurry up. You got to get the fire going.' She turned back to the window and carried on hammering.

'It's lumpy,' Frank said.

'You got to stir it harder.' Iris started on the other side of the window.

Frank rested the stick on the side of the bowl and wandered over to the fireplace. The stone inside the chimney was covered in thick black soot. Bending down, he peered up and saw the small piece of sky at the top. He began to lay the fire.

Iris finished and stood back to inspect her work. Two curtains were gathered down the sides. One, an old dress, had a small flower print and large white buttons. The other was mattress ticking, with a rough, unhemmed edge.

Iris adjusted the fabric until both sides were the same length, then took a spare piece of ticking and rubbed at the panes of glass until the worst of the dust and dirt disappeared.

Frank broke a peat turf into small pieces and added it to the paper and kindling.

Iris looked in the bowl. 'Call that finished?' She poured in more water and started mixing.

'We got to cook them today?' Frank asked.

'If you wanna play it, yeh.'

Frank took another turf off the pile. 'I don't wanna play it.'

'You do. You said you did.'

Frank threw the turf on the fire and stood up. 'I never

did.' He walked through to the next room. Shouted back at her, 'You always choose who to play.'

'You're gonna be king, stupid.'

'Only so you can hit me.' He shut the door between the two rooms.

The nest was by the window; the rest of the reed lay evenly on the mattress springs, covered in hessian sacks. The boot still lay on the earth floor, the stick still leant against the wall. Frank grabbed them both and slid them under the bed, shaking the cobwebs from his fingers.

He went back in the other room, where Iris was coming in from the scullery, carrying a heavy iron pan that she rested near the fire.

'Come on,' she said. 'Get it going.'

Frank bent down in front of the peat and kindling.

Iris took a handful of the oatmeal mixture and flattened it between her hands into a patty. Put it to one side and shaped another. And then another, until all the mixture was used up.

Frank watched the rush of flames on the turf. He balanced the pan on the edge of the fire.

'Wait till it dies down,' Iris said. 'Don't you know nothing?' She went into the scullery and Frank heard her moving things round.

He took a stick and scratched at the earth floor while he waited for the fire to settle, then returned the pan to the flames and let the metal heat through. Put the first patty on and watched it as it heated.

Iris came back. 'You have to turn them over.'

'When they're browned?' Frank asked.

'*Lightly* browned,' Iris said. She passed him a knife and he levered up the patty, tried to turn it over, but the mixture stuck to the pan so only the top of it came off, leaving a crust stuck to the metal. Iris pushed Frank away. 'Let me do it.'

Frank stood up. He looked over at the window, the lowering sun behind the orchard.

Iris shook her head and scraped at the burned bits. Brushed them into the flames. She fetched another patty to cook. 'Right. Let's try again.' She glanced at Frank. 'I'm getting tired. What with the baby and that.'

'What baby?'

Iris rested her hands in the small of her back, jutted her belly out.

'My baby,' she said.

'You haven't got a baby.'

'Not now. But I will do.'

'This another game?'

Iris stroked her belly, left her hands on it. 'It's in here.'

'What game is it?'

'Ain't a game.'

'Shut up.'

Iris grabbed his arm. 'You saying I'm lying?'

'I ain't saying nothing.'

'You'll see,' Iris said. 'You will.'

Frank shrugged.

'You're not to tell. About the house or the baby or any of it.'

'Ain't gonna tell.'

'Good. So we gonna play?'

'No. I wanna go on.'

'But the cakes.'

'Don't want to do it.'

'Well you wanna play summat else? You can be the robin and I'll be the foot-washer.'

Frank pulled his arm free of Iris's grasp. 'No. I'm going on.'

'Where?'

'Going to the field.'

'Can't keep away from Father?'

Iris threw the pan into the fire.

'You don't have to do that,' Frank said, stepping backwards towards the door.

Iris seized the remaining patties, and added them to the flames.

'I'll play tomorrow.' Frank stepped into the scullery. 'We'll make some more mixture.'

Iris stood glaring at the fire.

'And play the animals.'

Nothing.

'I'd've burned them anyway,' Frank said. 'If I'm the king.'

Iris looked at him. 'You never wanna come here.'

Frank shrugged.

'You scared?'

'Don't be stupid.'

'Well why don't you like it here?'

'I didn't say I don't.'

Iris stared at him for a while, then brushed past him, out into the sun.

Father walked towards them, along the grass drove. Frank ran to him and Father grabbed him under the arms, raising him high in the air, swinging him right round before putting him down again.

'Do that to me.' Iris reached her arms round his waist.

Father pushed her away. 'Too old for that now. Look at you.'

'I don't like getting old,' Iris said.

'There's not a lot we can do about that.' Father took Frank's hand and they started for home, the sun behind them.

'Where you been?' Father asked.

Frank looked across at Iris who glared at him. 'Nowhere much,' she said.

'And where's that?'

Iris ran on ahead. 'You know, everywhere.' She bent down and peered at something in the grass.

Father squeezed Frank's hand. 'You all right?'

Frank nodded. 'I was gonna come and help you in the field.'

'You can help tomorrow.'

Iris stopped and waited for them. 'You taking us to market tomorrow?' she asked.

Father shook his head. 'Better not leave your mother.'

'In case the baby comes?' Frank asked.

'That's it,' Father said. 'I was gonna take you to the abbey after the market, but I thought better of it.'

'Can we go another day?' Frank asked. 'After.'

'Yeh. I was gonna tell you the next story.'

'Can't you do it now?'

'Ought to save it for when we're there.'

'Is it about the abbey?' Iris asked.

'Yeh.'

'Is it true?' Frank asked.

'I wish it weren't,' Father said.

Dissolute Behaviour

Abbot Whiting stared up at the leaves, at the pattern they made against the blue sky. It was quite beautiful and if it weren't nearly midday he could stay and look at them for a very long time.

He glanced over at the abbey. Wondered at the size of it, built on the site of England's first wattle-and-daub church. Wondered at Joseph and his staff and the chalice, all those years ago. Wondered at the sheer holiness of the place. Wondered, as it was nearly midday, what the monks would be cooking for lunch. Eel, perhaps, with elderflower cordial. Or eggs – scotched, maybe. Or broken and then fried.

He wondered too, as he did on occasion, how much you would have to eat to end up the size of Henry VIII. A lot, he thought. What Henry needed was a few months here in Glastonbury Abbey. Silent meals and hard benches. Listening to the reading from the pulpit, signing for another slab of bread, only for the monk next to him to shake his head. Mouth silently, no, you've had enough, Your Royal Vastness.

The abbot smiled. To reach this state of power and grace and sit here on a bench looking at leaves, thinking these child-like thoughts. How lucky no one would know. No one except God, and He would forgive him. Abbot Whiting'd always been convinced of God's sense of humour. You couldn't be alive and not see what a joke it all was. On a good day, anyway.

The abbot stood. His knees ached. You couldn't be alive, either, and reach your seventies with no physical sign of ageing. A shame. All this wisdom and the body falling apart around you. He set off towards the abbey. Observing every leaf, every bird, every scrap of nature he could. He was making the most of each day, knowing the trap set by Thomas Crumwell, Henry VIII's adviser, was closing. Years of reforms, designed to make life difficult. And the abbot had managed those, responding with his well-known patience. But now it was getting serious, so serious it threatened his rather particular approach: tolerance; humour; utter honesty.

He had seen the new Act, penned by Crumwell: Henry VIII will seize any religious house where treason has taken place.

Treason. Just a word. And yet how flexible. Words were like that, Abbot Whiting found. Flexible and variable in definition. In the beginning was the word and the word was subject to interpretation, not to mention translation.

He reached the refectory.

A spot of eel would go down very well indeed. Perhaps with some eggs. And a cut tomato.

Crumwell chose Dr Layton to be his messenger. Sent him to Glastonbury, to visit Abbot Whiting at his home on the edge of the flat land.

Layton was shown into the study by a silent monk; Abbot Whiting was bent over his desk, writing. Hair silver in the September sun.

He blotted his paper, then looked up. 'Take a seat, Dr Layton.'

Layton sat.

'I thought you might be coming to see me.'

Layton nodded. 'I'm here to ask some questions.'

'Which I will, of course, answer.' Abbot Whiting looked Layton directly in the eye. 'I have no fear of you.' He put his palms together as though in prayer. 'I want you to know something. God sees through me as if I am made of glass. I hide nothing.'

Layton looked at the desk, tried to see the paper. 'My men are in your abbey.'

Abbot Whiting shrugged. 'They'll find nothing against me.'

A pause.

'You're not a young man.'

Whiting smiled.

'You are nearing your eightieth year.'

'That is correct.'

'And perhaps you are not a healthy man.'

'Thank you for your concern. Most appreciated.'

Layton shrugged. There was silence for a while, then one of Layton's men entered the room. Whispered and handed over some papers.

Abbot Whiting watched while Layton read them.

'So,' Layton said eventually. He pushed the papers across the desk. Abbot Whiting scanned them. Looked up.

'You ask me to sign over my abbey?' He gestured at one of the sheets. 'You ask me to sign this?'

'You are an intelligent man, my lord Abbot. You know you should sign.'

'And you say you found these other papers in my possession.'

'We did.'

'Then I have a difficulty. You see, Layton, as I have told you, I am transparent before my God. He knows that I have

121

never previously seen these papers. If I sign and hand over my abbey, I will be betraying him.'

'Sign, your lordship.'

'And if I do not sign, then I am accusing my king's men of lying.'

'Enough talk. Sign.'

'Not a pretty choice, but a clever one.'

'Do you admit to treason?'

'I have committed no acts of treason.'

Layton stood and went to the door. Spoke to one of his men who passed him three books.

Layton sat down. Handed the books to Abbot Whiting.

'We found these at the abbey.'

Abbot Whiting opened one, read a passage. 'I don't know this book. Nor this.'

Layton smiled. 'I think you do.'

Abbot Whiting shook his head. 'And even if I knew this book, is there an Act of Parliament which bans me from reading it?'

'Silence.' His voice, loud. A pause, then, 'You will see the books contain written arguments against the royal divorce.'

Abbot Whiting gazed steadily at Layton. 'I have not seen this before.'

'Sign the paper, my lord Abbot.'

'No.'

'Right.' Layton stood. 'In that case, we go to London.'

'And in London?'

'We shall discuss these acts of treason.'

'If that is what you want.'

Layton smiled. 'It is late and a long way to London. You are an old man. You choose to make this journey?'

Whiting sat back in his chair. He closed his eyes for a second, then opened them. 'I do not choose it.'

'Then sign.'

A long pause.

'So.' Layton nodded. 'We shall go to London.'

And so it was that the Abbot of Glastonbury was taken to London, to the Tower, and placed in a cell.

He lay on the stone bench and closed his eyes. Saw again the pattern of leaves against the blue sky.

How simple life would be if he did what others wanted. But he couldn't. He rolled over. Pulled the blanket up to his chin and slept.

The next morning, after he had eaten his bowl of porridge, the door opened and the guard ushered a man into the cell, closed the door behind him.

'My lord Abbot?'

'Crumwell.'

Crumwell smiled. 'This is not a place for an old man.'

'I didn't notice.'

'I could take you back to Somerset. Give you a house, a pension, a competent cook. One who can prepare eel as you like it. Squeeze cordial from an elderflower. You could live the rest of your life in comfort.'

'And in exchange?'

Crumwell laughed. 'Why make it hard for yourself?'

'In exchange you would ask for the abbey.'

'You can be a stupid man,' Crumwell said.

'Not stupid, but honest. I admit it's not a great attribute. Look where it's brought me.'

'You don't have to be here.'

'You don't seem to understand. I have no choice.'

Crumwell paced the length of the cell. 'Let's talk of evidence. The books Layton discovered.'

'The books I had not seen.'

'The books and the plate my men found hidden in the abbey.'

'There was nothing hidden.'

'Your treasurer, John Thorne, and sacristan, Roger James, are imprisoned in the gatehouse.'

'My men are not thieves. You know that.'

'Enough,' Crumwell shouted. 'We have evidence. You are just an old man. An old man in the way.' He banged on the cell door and it opened. 'You have twenty-four hours to think about it.' Crumwell left.

Abbot Whiting spent the twenty-four hours in prayer.

At dawn, Crumwell entered the cell. He stood in the doorway.

'So, your lordship?'

Abbot Whiting shook his head. 'I can't hand over the abbey.'

'You betray your king.'

'I cannot betray my God. You see, if I confess to these false accusations, I lie. I have chosen the truth.'

'You have chosen to make a martyr of yourself?'

'I'm not after glory. I am just an old man, as you said. An old man with a simple faith. No more than that.'

'A stupid old man.'

Abbot Whiting smiled. 'There is nothing more to say.'

And so the abbot was loaded in a cart and driven to the palace at Wells, where he was met by a public audience and a jury, ready to charge him. People rushed forward with false accusations as he stood with burglars and rapists and waited for the carefully selected jury to declare him guilty, as requested by Crumwell.

As soon as sentence was passed, Whiting was taken to

Glastonbury to await his punishment. It was dark by the time he was locked in the abbey gatehouse. While the abbot slept, the two men with him, John Thorne and Roger James, prayed.

They came at dawn. Took them out into the grey November morning, into the street by the abbey, where they had already spread hurdles across the road. They laid the men on the woven wood and tied them down, then attached the hurdles to horses and dragged them through the town in front of large crowds, back past the abbey.

Here, they stopped the horses so Abbot Whiting could see the stripped roof, the carts being loaded with silver. The stream of smoke rising from the fire where the books burned. When they decided he had seen enough, they urged the horses forward.

The first drops of rain fell as they headed out of the town towards the Tor. The horses pulled over the wet grass, up the hill; the crowd followed.

At the top they untied the three men, but the abbot could not move, for his bones were broken. He could still see though, could see what had been erected on the top of the hill.

Three crosses.

Three wooden crucifixes outlined against the sky. Against the grey clouds.

The men were taken, one at a time, to the three crosses.

Still the rain fell. The rain fell and the sky darkened and from his cross Abbot Whiting looked down at the town, at the hill where Joseph planted his staff, at the well where the chalice lay, deep in the water, at the green flat land beyond. The land which stretched to the sea.

The wind blew and the birds fell silent.

'Have you anything to say?'

Abbot Whiting spoke his final words: 'I ask forgiveness of my God and king for anything I have done.'

The three men were left to suffer on their crosses. The holy man. The two thieves.

Abbot Whiting's lips moved as he prayed silently. He imagined the rain falling on his body becoming blood, running down the cross, sinking into the wet ground, feeding the grass.

The sky darkened, became black. He wanted the earth to shake, rupture. Wanted the saints to climb from their graves and walk through Glastonbury. He closed his eyes.

Died.

The corpses were cut down and Abbot Whiting's body divided into four, the quarters sent to Wells, Bath, Ilchester and Bridgwater.

His head was fixed to the gates of the abbey. Inside the fires burned and men broke the bells and packed the scrap into barrels, ready for the speculator's bid.

The rain continued to fall and one manuscript fell from the fire, landing in a pool of water, where the illuminated letters started to blur.

∽

There was silence in the house when they got back. A loaf on the table. Four plates. A jug on its side. Milk on the floor, a white pool caught between the flagstones.

Father called out. 'Hello.'

They heard a voice upstairs and Father ran up the curved stone steps. Frank stared at the milk.

'Iris. Get help,' Father shouted from the bedroom.

Iris stared at Frank.

'Quick,' he called down. 'Go now.'

Iris ran out of the back door. Frank watched a drop of milk fall from the jug's spout.

Later, after help had arrived, Father righted the jug. He used a rag to mop up the worst of the milk on the floor.

Frank looked at Iris, who walked into the scullery, then out of the back door.

'What's going on?' Frank asked.

'We got to wait.' Father carried the rag into the scullery and rinsed it in the bowl in the sink until the water became dirty white, then he wiped the floor again.

Frank watched for a while, then went outside. He walked through the garden to the vegetable plot, where he lay in the long grass and stared back at the house. At the upstairs windows.

The sky darkened and he waited for the stars.

Waited.

Then Iris was there, standing over him.

'Getting late,' she said.

'I know.'

'Father says you got to come in.'

Frank looked at her. 'Is the baby here yet?'

Iris turned and walked back to the house. Frank stood up and followed.

Father was at the table. 'Bed.'

'Is it here yet?' Frank asked.

'Maybe by morning.'

Frank and Iris climbed the stairs to their room.

Father called up, 'Close your door.'

Iris walked to the open window and looked out.

A scream. Another scream.

'What's happening?' Frank asked.

Iris spoke without turning round. 'Shut up.'

Frank looked at her back for a while, then took off his shirt and got into bed. Closed his eyes.

He woke in the night and reached across to touch Iris, but the bed was empty, Iris gone.

He fell back asleep, back into his dreams.

Iris swimming in the rhyne, deep under green duckweed. Her white skin in the dark water. Her head coming up, the head of a seal, dark hair wet. And Frank on the bank of the rhyne, thinking he would never see her again, but Iris coming up through the water, laughing, duckweed clinging to her body. Iris staring at him, then saying she lived in the land where the dead rose: Jesus, King Arthur, Joseph's stick.

And Frank sitting on the bank of the rhyne, a butterfly in his hand, a common blue. And the butterfly turning to Frank and saying, 'Wake up. Wake up.'

~

Screaming, the butterfly on his face. Wings draped over his nose, stopping up his nostrils, stopping him breathing.

Iris in the water. The green duckweed on her skin.

'Shush, Dad. You're pulling it out.'

'What's he doing?'

'Leave the room, George. Go and see Brian.'

No air. No water. The grass dry and the pollen choking him.

'That's it, just lie still.'

And Iris.

~

Frank woke in the morning. The sun fell through the window, and he stretched out. His leg went right across the bed instead of meeting the hot body of his sister. He looked around. The covers, thrown back. Iris, gone still. He sat up. Listened. Nothing. He got out of bed, pulled his clothes on, went out onto the landing.

His mother's door was closed and he stood there for a while, then went down the stairs, running his hand along the curved wall. There was bread on the table. A glass of water. The fire was out, hadn't been lit. He walked into the scullery. The bowl in the sink, the dirty rag in the grey water. He looked out of the back door, to where Father stood against the wall, smoking his pipe.

Father turned and grinned. 'Sleep well?'

'What's happened?'

'You better go and see.'

Frank ran back inside and up the stairs. Opened the door to his mother's room.

She lay back against the pillows. Her eyes closed.

Frank stood, his hand on the latch. He saw the pile of sheets in the corner, stained red-brown. Saw the wicker crib standing by the window.

Mother opened her eyes. Smiled. Whispered, 'Have a look.'

She nodded towards the crib and he walked over quietly. Bent down over it, saw it wrapped in a sheet and a blanket. Its tiny head and one hand. Fingers fanned out.

He stared for a long time.

'What is it?' he whispered.

'A baby,' she said. He stared at her and she laughed. 'A girl,' she said. 'A sister.'

'C'I touch her?'

'Course you can. Just be gentle.'

Frank reached out and touched her finger with his. Felt the skin of her. He looked at his mother. 'You pleased?' she asked.

Frank nodded.

'Come and sit by me,' she said.

He looked at the baby once again, then walked over and perched on the bed.

'I'll teach you to hold her when she wakes up.'

'When will she?'

'When she wants milk again.'

'How does she know?'

'Spec her tummy starts rumbling.'

'She ain't very big,' Frank said.

'Babies aren't.'

They sat for a while, then Frank asked, 'She got a name?'

'Not yet. What d'you reckon?'

Frank shrugged. 'Dunno.'

'We'll wait and see what suits her, eh?'

'Yeh.' Frank looked around the room. 'You getting up now?'

Mother smiled. 'Gonna have a bit of a rest.'

'Why d'you need a rest?'

'Bit tiring.'

'Why?'

'Just is.'

'Oh.' Frank tapped his fingers on his lap, then stood up.

'Where you off to?' Mother asked.

'Has Iris seen her yet?'

'She wouldn't come in.' Mother glanced over at the window. 'Needs a bit of time.'

'She gone out?'

'Dunno where she is. Father told her she's got to stay around and help me for the day.'

'Right.' Frank walked over to the crib and pulled the sheet away from her face. Saw the pale eyelids. The dark hairs on her ears. 'She's hairy.'

'It's normal,' Mother said. 'It'll come off.'

'Better had, or they'll give her hell at school.'

Mother laughed. 'She'll be all right, don't you worry.'

'Yeh. Spec she will.'

'When you see Iris, ask if she'll get the fire going, make some tea.'

Frank nodded. 'See you later.' Mother smiled and he left.

Father handed Frank the metal bucket. 'C'you manage? I got to get on.'

Frank nodded. He stood in the sun holding the warm handle.

'Yeh,' Father said. 'I got to get on.'

Frank watched him go to the end of their land and cross the sleeper bridge over the rhyne into the field beyond.

Frank placed the bucket beside the cow. Brought the stool over and sat by her, pushed his head against her hot flank. Flies landed on her, then slowly lifted into the air, landed again. Frank grasped her warm teats and started pulling until milk flowed into the bucket. When he was finished, he took the bucket into the scullery, stopping to get a few leaves of mint to add to the milk so it wouldn't go off.

Outside the hens scratched in the dust and he chased the smallest one for a bit, until he caught her and she settled down for him to stroke. He picked her up. The scales on her legs were raised, and some had peeled away, revealing her pink skin beneath. She clawed at him and he let her fly to the ground where she shook her feathers and ran off.

He wandered past the allotment to the bridge. Knelt down by the water, put his hand in and stirred the weed. He pulled out a newt, solid in his hand, a strong body. He watched it curl up slowly, then turned it over and looked at the pattern on its belly, stroked the ridge down its back and put it back in the water. It swam to the bottom.

131

A damselfly settled on the surface of the water.

The empty bed, in the night. Iris missing. The dream of her in the water. In the rhyne.

Frank stood up.

He knew where she'd be. He'd get her, bring her back to help Mother.

He climbed the gate into the orchard, walked through the long grass and trees to their house. Through the scullery, into the middle room.

Iris knelt on the floor, something in the folds of her dress. Frank stood and watched as she rubbed it and then placed it beside her.

The edge was still stained with earth, but Frank could see the blue and white pattern. Broken china.

Iris looked up. 'I found it digging. Found loads of them.'

She tipped the contents of her skirt onto the earth floor and started sorting the pieces into piles: blue and white, natural, plain white and glass.

'What were you digging for?'

'Merlin's coffin.'

Frank waited.

'I keep searching for the gold in the peat.'

'But it could be anywhere.'

Iris shrugged.

'The moors go right to the sea.'

'I know.'

'It's another game, isn't it?' Frank asked.

Iris picked up a green shard of glass, started cleaning it.

'It is,' Frank said. His voice too loud. 'It's just a game.'

Iris looked up. Pale eyes and dark hair. She stared at him, then carried on polishing.

'Iris.' She looked up again. 'I don't like these games.'

Iris shrugged. 'You said it's just a game.'

Frank waited. 'You weren't at home. I woke in the night and you'd gone.'

She held the fragment up to inspect it, then placed it on the glass pile.

'You been here in the night, haven't you?'

She bent down, her hair covering her face.

'You can't do that,' Frank said. 'It ain't right.'

Iris swept her hand through her carefully heaped pieces and they scattered across the floor.

Silence, then Iris leant over and started picking them up. Sorted them back into their piles, then stood up. Left the room.

Frank knelt down on the earth floor and reached out a finger to touch a triangle of white china. The spout of a small jug.

Iris returned, her skirt tucked up. She knelt down and unfolded the material and another pile of china fell to the floor.

'What game is it you're doing?' Frank asked.

'I'm not telling.' She lifted one piece of glass up to the light: a bottle neck with a glass ball in it, black earth stuck inside.

'Iris.'

'What?'

'I went to see the baby.'

'What baby?'

'Stop it.' Frank felt his voice crack.

'You gonna cry?'

Frank turned away.

'They know you're here?'

Frank shook his head.

'You told them about the house?'

'No.'

'Good.' Iris smiled. 'It's all right, Frank.' She pointed at some brown china. 'I spec people ate out of this.'

'Maybe.'

'Maybe they ate pelican.'

Frank shook his head.

'You don't reckon?'

'That was before proper houses.'

Iris nodded. 'You're right.'

'There wouldn't have been pelicans when they lived here.'

'No. See, you ain't stupid. You wanna be the robin?'

Frank shrugged.

'You don't wanna play?'

'Mother says she wants some tea. Says you're to light the fire.'

Iris turned away.

'She said I'm to get you.'

Iris placed her hands in the small of her back. 'I want to show you summat.'

'What?'

She laid one hand on her belly. 'Put your hand here.'

Frank looked towards the scullery. 'She'll be waiting. She's there with the baby.'

Iris grabbed his arm and pulled his hand towards her belly. 'Put it there, you'll feel it moving.'

Frank jerked away, ran to the scullery door. He looked back. 'I hate it here,' he said. And he left.

She lay in bed, propped up against the bolster which she'd folded in two. A striped sheet covering her. The baby lay in her arms, against her chest.

'I brought you bread and butter,' Frank said.

'Thanks.'

'Shall I put it on the bed?'

134

Mother nodded.

Frank put the plate beside her, on top of the sheet. Sat the other side of her.

He could see the baby's hand dangling out of the shawl. Her fingers.

'You all right?'

Frank nodded.

'You found Iris?'

'She's coming.'

'She all right? She say anything about the baby?'

'No.'

'She'll come round. She will.'

Frank nodded. 'You thought of any names?'

Mother shook her head. 'One'll come. Wait long enough and it makes itself known.'

Frank looked at her hands. Red skin, tiny nails, ragged at the ends.

'Where was Iris?'

'Just out playing.' As he spoke, the baby's head moved. 'What's she doing?' But then he saw her mouth open, saw his mother's breast, taut skin with blue veins and hard red nipple. White drip of milk.

He looked away, quickly. Looked down at the floor.

'That's it,' he heard Mother say. 'There it is.'

The noise of sucking. Swallowing.

'There's a good little girl.'

Frank glanced up at the doorway, at the open door, and saw Iris standing there, watching.

~

Frank opened his eyes.

The fire had almost gone out. There was another wooden chair by the bed.

Feet on the stairs. He waited and watched the door open.

Brian walked in sideways holding the tray. Pushed the door closed and slid the tray onto the floor. Walked to the fire and picked up pieces of coal, one at a time, and placed them on the burning embers. Rubbed his hand on his jeans. Sat down. Yawned, drummed his fingers on his lap.

'You tired?' Frank asked.

Brian jumped. 'I thought you were asleep.'

'Not now.'

Brian smiled. 'Brought some tea up, but I didn't wanna wake you.'

'What time is it?'

'Past midnight.'

Brian bent down and poured the tea.

'Margaret'll be up in a minute.'

'You wanna be getting on to bed.'

'We're all right,' Brian said.

'Bloody late.'

'Yeh, well. Nice with the fire lit,' he said. 'Must take you back.'

No answer.

'You had this room before, didn't you? When you were a young'un.'

'Always had this room.'

'Well,' Brian said. 'You travelled a long way, Frank. That room to this one.'

'Far enough,' Frank said. 'People now, never happy.'

'No.'

'We had no need of a lot.'

'No.'

'A roof. Bit of work.'

Brian picked up the tea and sipped. He put it down. 'I'll leave yours for a bit,' he said. 'Let it cool some more.'

'Spec you miss the work,' Frank said.

136

The new coals started to catch and flames rose in the fireplace.

Brian nodded. 'Sometimes.'

Margaret put her head around the door, came in and sat on the other chair. She tucked her hair behind her ears. 'That cup for me?'

'It's your dad's.'

'I don't want any,' Frank said.

'Go on,' Brian said. 'Do you good, bit of sugar.'

Frank shook his head. 'You have it.'

Margaret shrugged and took the cup, holding it in both hands, looking at Frank.

'You sure you're all right?'

Frank nodded. 'Funny. I remembered something that happened.'

Margaret leant forward.

'I'd forgotten about it.' Frank looked at the fire.

Margaret waited.

'One day we were digging down by Lower Drove. The spade hit something and we stopped. Dug it out.'

Margaret sat back.

'A dead pelican?' Brian suggested.

'You soft bugger,' Frank said. 'It was a wooden bowl. Still had these nuts in it. That's what got me. From all those years ago and the nuts still in it.'

Brian shook his head. 'Never understood why they lived down here in the wet.'

Frank looked at Brian. 'You live down here.'

'Bugger.' Brian laughed. 'I do too.'

'You wouldn't live anywhere else,' Margaret said. 'You told me.'

'Never did.'

'You know you did.'

'Maybe after I'd had a few.'

'Maybe,' Margaret said, 'but you still said it.'

'Yeh, well. Not such a bad old place. I wouldn't wanna eat pelicans mind, you'd be spitting bones for a week.'

Frank laughed. 'Getting late,' he said. 'You wanna be going on to bed, Margaret.'

'Yeh,' Margaret said. She put her cup down. 'Dad?'

'Yeh.'

'You were talking earlier, you know. You said . . .' Margaret hesitated. 'You said something about a baby. Was the baby Iris?'

A long silence.

Frank looked down at the bed, ran his finger along the groove in the counterpane, between the tufts.

'No.'

'What happened?'

'Margaret,' Brian said.

Margaret looked at him.

'That's enough,' he said quietly.

No one spoke for a while, then Brian stretched. 'Reckon I might try and get some sleep.' He bent down and picked up the tray. 'Night, then.'

'Night,' Frank said.

'You coming?' Brian asked Margaret.

'In a minute.'

'Right. Well don't be long. Your dad needs some sleep. Sleep and *peace*.'

Margaret twisted her wedding ring round.

'I'm all right,' Frank said.

'I thought we were losing you, Dad.'

'Don't be soft.'

'You're all right now?'

138

'I'm fine. It's just the medicine.' Frank lifted his arm, nodded at the drip.

'Does it still hurt?'

Frank nodded.

'Then have some more. Press the button. They said whenever you needed it.'

'I know what they said.'

'You don't like it, do you?'

'Makes me feel queer.'

'We'll talk to them in the morning, when they come, see if there's anything else they can do.'

'Don't want them to come.'

'I know.'

Frank was silent for a while. Then, 'Reckon you ought to get some sleep.'

'Yeh.' Margaret stood up, pushing her hair away from her face. 'I am a bit tired, to be honest. Let's do your pillows.' She removed the two top ones and laid the others flat, helped lay Frank back against them.

'See if you can get a good night's sleep now.'

'Yeh.'

Margaret reached a hand out towards her father, then pulled it back. She rested it on the counterpane, then patted it. 'I'll see you in the morning, Dad.'

Frank nodded.

'Fire all right like that?' The last coals were burning quietly.

'It's fine.'

'Right.'

Margaret smoothed the counterpane, then turned out the light and left the room.

Fen Peat

Frank looked up at the underside of the table. He reached out and touched the rough wood with his finger. His skin caught and he pulled back. A tiny splinter, sticking out. He took the fragment of wood between his nails and eased it out, leaving a hollow under the skin.

He watched Iris's legs as she stood by the fire, one leg tucked behind the other, one foot rubbing the back of her calf. She had a bite, red with fresh blood where she'd been scratching.

Frank heard feet coming down the stairs. Glimpsed Father's legs and his bare feet, dark with dirt. Long toes with hairs on them.

'You lit the fire, then.'

'Yeh,' Iris said.

'You seen Frank?'

'No.'

A pause, then Father. 'You been to see her?'

'I'm making her tea.'

'You know what I'm saying.'

Silence.

'Iris.'

More silence.

Frank pulled his knees up to his chin and wrapped his arms around them. He rocked slowly, back and forth.

'She's your sister.'

He saw Iris bend down, scratch her leg. More blood.

'You gonna say what's on?'

'Ain't nothing on,' Iris said.

'So why don't you wanna see her?'

'Don't have to do anything.'

The sound of the kettle.

Frank smelled his knees. Earth. And skin.

Iris's legs moved away from the fire, out of the room. Father's followed.

From the scullery, 'Can't go on like this,' Father said.

'I dunno what you're on about.'

'Your mother. You'll upset her.'

'Can't help that.'

Her legs back in. The kettle boiling on the fire. The sound of the water swilling around the pot, then being tipped into the fire. The hiss of the flames.

Tea leaves. Water. The pot resting on the trivet.

Father's legs by the door.

'So that's it. You ain't got nothing to say.'

Nothing.

'Carry on like this, I ought to take a strap to you.'

'Like to see you try.'

'Been too bloody soft, I have.'

Father walking towards the stairs. 'I'll give it a day,' he said, 'and after that you'd better've stopped all this.'

His feet going. Iris standing there, saying softly, 'Give it a day, and you'd better've stopped all this.'

Tea, poured into cups.

Her legs going out of the room.

He waited until Father's legs came back. Waited as they

144

stood by the table while Father drank his tea. He watched them leave.

Frank crawled out from under the table and into the scullery. He tipped one of the buckets of milk: the thick, sour skin clung to the side; the mint leaves were black, and the milk beneath thin and pale.

He watched an ant walk across the floor by his knees. Saw another following, then a whole row of them, all in a line, coming from outside.

Iris was down by the hens.

He tracked the ants to their nest outside in the dry grass. Poked a finger in the powdered earth so the ants rushed out and ran in circles.

Father walked up to him. 'There you are. Come and get summat to eat. We're off in a minute.'

Frank brushed an ant off his hand. 'Where we going?'

'I'm taking you digging.'

Frank stood up. 'Is Iris coming?'

Father shook his head. 'She's gonna stay here.'

'And Mum? Is she getting up today?'

'She'll be up soon, I spec. Come on.'

In the long trench where the peat had been dug out, the sides of it showed the layers, from the topsoil down to the rich, black peat. The row of ruckles on the side, the men lifting turves onto them to dry. The sound of spades and the voices, calling out.

Frank laid the turves out in the crucifix for the base of the hyle.

Father stood talking to two men. As Frank moved on to the next hyle, Father finished his conversation and walked over. 'Getting on all right?'

The sun was in Frank's eyes and he couldn't see Father's face. 'Yeh.'

Father adjusted one of the turves. 'Got to get the base firm. Or it'll topple.'

Frank finished the cross and started building the turves on top.

Father watched him closely. 'So,' he said. 'What d'you reckon to the baby?'

'She's all right.'

'Iris said anything to you?'

'No.'

Father picked up a wet turf and placed it on the hyle. 'Looks good,' he said. 'Nice and strong now.'

Frank started another, laid out the turves.

'So,' Father said, 'she ain't said anything to you about the baby, then?'

'No.'

'Right.'

Father watched Frank finish the hyle, then walked back to the men and started digging.

They sat at the table that evening. A pan of potatoes. A plate of cheese: deep yellow beneath a film of sweat. Four radishes on each plate, and a boiled egg, sliced in two. The yolk with a grey line round the outside. The solid white.

Frank picked up his knife and poked it into a crack in the table, loosening the dirt.

'Mother all right today?' Father asked Iris.

Iris nodded.

'Good.'

Frank pressed the dirt back into the crack.

'So, you seen the baby then?'

Iris said nothing. Looked at her plate.

'You got till tomorrow. You hear?'

'You said a day,' Iris said.

'That's tomorrow.'

'Depends when you're counting from.'

'That's enough.' Father pulled the breadboard towards him and starting cutting slices. 'We all just got to settle down.'

'Can I have some bread?' Frank held out his hand and Father passed him a slice.

'So,' Father said. 'I've got a surprise for you two tomorrow. Gonna take you somewhere.'

'Where?' Frank asked.

'Wait and see. You'll like it, eh, Iris?'

'Maybe,' Iris said.

'You will, girl.' Father held one of the plates out. 'You wanna take this up?'

'She can come down,' Iris said.

Silence for a moment.

'I said, you gonna take it up.'

'I'll take it,' Frank grabbed the plate and walked up the stairs.

Mother got him to sit on the bed, his back against the bolster. He held his arms ready and she walked to the crib, picked up the baby, carried her to Frank. He reached out and she turned the bundle and placed her in his outstretched arms, keeping one hand there to support her head. She moved Frank's arm slightly then took her hand away. 'That all right?'

Frank nodded. He looked down at her face, and Mother pulled the shawl away so he could see more easily. Her eyes were closed, their lids pale. She turned her face towards him. 'She's moving.'

Mother put her hands under his arms. 'It's all right. Sit still.'

'What's she doing?' The baby's mouth, a small blister on her lower lip. Her eyes, open now. Pale blue.

'Just looking round, wondering who you are.'

'She know who I am?'

'I told her,' Mother said. 'Told her you're her big brother.'

'Hope she listened. Hope she can hear with that hair on her ears.'

'She listened. Doesn't wanna be in trouble with her brother already.'

Frank looked up at Mother. 'Why doesn't Iris wanna see her?'

Mother shrugged. 'Some people take a bit of time to take to a baby.'

Frank nodded.

'You all right holding her?'

'She's yawning. Didn't know they could yawn.'

The baby's mouth, stretched open. Greedy red inside. Pink tongue.

'Course they can yawn.'

'She's moving again.'

'You want me to take her back?'

Frank nodded. Mother lifted her from his arms, put her back in the crib. Sat on the bed next to Frank.

'Better eat this food you brought me up, eh?'

Frank stood up. 'I'd better go and eat mine.'

'Ain't you eaten yet?'

Frank shook his head.

'Go on, then.'

Frank nodded. Walked to the crib and peered in again, then went downstairs.

Bed that night, and Frank with the covers off. Hot. The candle flame burning down near the saucer.

'Iris,' he said.

Her back to him. 'What?'

A pause. Then, 'D'you wish the baby was yours?'

She didn't answer for a long time, then she sat up. 'That story Father told us. The first story.'

'In the field.'

'That boy in it, Jesus,' she said. 'He was born in the straw. Just came to her.'

'An angel gave it her.'

'Like my baby.'

'I don't like this game,' Frank said.

'My belly's all stretched.' Iris stood and pulled up her dress. Frank saw the belly button, the flat belly, the few black hairs round her slit. Looked away quickly.

'Look,' Iris said. 'See how it sticks out.'

'Stop it.'

'Thing is, Frank, when this baby comes, you'll see you're wrong. Ain't gonna be long now.'

'I hate this game.'

'Did I say it was a game?'

'I know it's a game.'

Iris knelt down on the bed. Got close to Frank's ear. Whispered. 'It ain't a game.'

Frank put his head under the pillow. The candle light faded and died.

When he woke later, he found the bed empty.

In the morning, Iris was there again, and he didn't know if his waking had been a dream.

Father drove the pony and cart, Frank and Iris sitting in the back on the thin layer of peat, where the turves had lain. Through Westonzoyland and down onto the moors. Father stopped the cart at Bussex Farm. 'Here we are,' Father said. He tethered the pony and Frank and Iris got out.

Father took a small wicker basket from the cart.

'Where are we?' Iris asked.

Father took Frank's hand. 'Come and see this.'

Iris stood by the cart while Father and Frank set off through the farmyard. After a few steps, Father stopped and looked back.

'Come on, Iris.'

Iris ran to catch them up.

They walked until they reached a field where a small area of grass had been fenced off, a granite memorial standing in the centre of four stone mushrooms. Two young poplar trees stood either side, their trunks in iron callipers, their leaves changing from green to white as they caught in the light breeze.

Father read the words aloud.

> To the Glory of God
> And in Memory of All Those Who
> Doing the Right as they Gave it
> Fell in the Battle of Sedgemoor
> 6th July 1685
> And Lie Buried in this Field
> or Who for their Share in the Fight
> Suffered Death
> Punishment or Transportation
> Pro Patria.

'I don't understand,' Frank said.

Father rested the basket on the ground and sat beside it.

He took out a paper-wrapped slab of bread and some cheese and apples. 'Sit down,' he said.

Iris knelt on the grass.

Father took his knife from his pocket and cut the bread into three.

'What's it mean?' Frank asked.

Father handed him his bread and a slice of cheese. 'I'm gonna tell you.'

All the King's Men

In Bussex Farm, Westonzoyland, back in the year 1685, there lived a woman and her husband. The woman's sister was widowed and thrown out of her house. The farmer's wife persuaded and wheedled until the farmer gave in and the sister came to live with them, though he knew as soon as he said oh all right then that he would regret it very much indeed.

In the evenings, when the cattle were fed, and the milking done, the farmer would come inside and sit in his chair by the fire. He liked to put his feet up and listen to the kettle boiling. He liked to nod off in the flickering light.

The first night after the sister moved in, he came into the house and found her sitting at the table, a pile of cakes in front of her.

He sat down in his chair and his wife brought him a drink.

'Well?' the sister said.

The farmer looked over. She sat behind her cakes, gesturing at them.

He waited.

'Well?' she said again.

'What do you want?'

She snorted.

The farmer's wife said, 'Tell her they look good.'

'Why do I have to do that?'

'She's particular about her cakes. She likes people to notice them.'

'Well, that's just bloody daft and I've had a hard day in the field.'

The sister banged her hand on the table. 'I made these cakes. I mixed butter and sugar and eggs, and put flour in. You say you've had a hard day. What about me?'

There was silence for a moment, then the farmer's wife said, 'Look, just say they're lovely cakes and then we can get on with the eating of them.'

The farmer settled back in his chair. 'You say they're lovely.'

'I already did. I know her ways.'

'Now look,' the farmer said. 'Let's get this quite straight.' He pointed at his wife. 'You want your sister here, you can have her here, but this house runs along my ways, not anyone else's.'

The sister picked up one of the cakes and threw it at the farmer. It missed and landed in the fire.

'We all have our own ways,' she said. 'I ain't gonna change mine to yours.'

'Now look.' The farmer put his hands on the arms of his chair, lifting himself up, looking at that pile of cakes on the table.

And there was a knock at the door.

The wife answered it and a young man pushed past her, came into the room and closed the door behind him.

'Well?' the farmer asked.

The man leant against the door while he caught his breath.

'Perhaps you'd like a cake,' the sister said.

'The king,' the man panted. 'Monmouth.'

'Come on, spit it out,' the farmer said. 'We got business here to do with these damned cakes.'

The wife took the man's arm. Guided him to a chair. 'Start at the beginning.'

The man nodded. He sat and then started. 'The Duke of Monmouth landed at Lyme Regis. He's in Taunton and they've declared him king.'

'Now that's just daft,' the sister said. 'There's already a king.'

'Let the man speak,' the farmer said.

'Well, there is. There's King James the number two.'

'The second,' the farmer's wife corrected.

'Second, number two, it's all the same to me,' the sister said.

The farmer shouted, 'I said, let him speak.'

The sister picked up another cake and threw it at the farmer. It bounced off his head and left small yellow crumbs on his hair.

'Take no notice.' The farmer brushed some of the crumbs onto his shoulders.

'I'll try not to,' the man said. 'So the men are gathering. The king's men.'

'Which king?' the sister asked.

'Shut up, woman,' the farmer said.

'Well, you see, it's gonna cause problems, calling them both the king.'

'So,' the farmer said, 'the *new* king's men are gathering and they're getting closer.'

'Right,' the man said.

The farmer glared at the sister. 'And you're going to fight for the *new* king?'

The man nodded.

'Well. What do you want from me?'

'We need men.'

'Ah,' the farmer said. 'I see.'

'Two and a half thousand men, the king has.'

'Which king would that be?' the sister asked.

'And Monmouth? How many men has he got?'

'A few more than that.'

'I see,' the farmer said. He sat without speaking for a while, in his comfy chair, by the fire, with the sound of the flames and the flickering light. Then he looked over at the table, at his wife's sister, arms folded behind her pile of cakes.

He stood up. 'We better go, then.'

'You're going to fight?' his wife asked.

The farmer stood by the man. 'Yes,' he said. 'I'm going to fight.'

The sister smiled, the wife cried, and the farmer and the man left the house.

Some days later, the farmer was resting on the bench at the church in Bridgwater. He'd walked too far and was tired. He put his feet up and leant back, and for a second he was in his favourite chair, the fire going and the kettle whispering.

But the man who'd encouraged him to join the army shook his shoulder. 'We're off.'

The farmer jumped. He saw Monmouth striding out of the church, spyglass in hand.

'He's seen the king's men at Westonzoyland, camping down for the night.'

'And we're going to surprise them?' the farmer asked.

'You know,' the man said, 'for a farmer you're not slow, are you?'

And they joined the men and slowly and quietly approached the edge of the moor where they hid, the farmer digging himself deep into the dry rhyne. He leant against the bank and, as the light faded, closed his eyes. There he was again, back in his kitchen. The wife at his side, her sister nowhere to be seen.

155

The man nudged him and passed him a pistol. 'Hold this,' he whispered and crawled to the top of the rhyne where he balanced his spyglass on the grass. Looked through it.

The farmer looked at the thing in his hand. He'd never held such a thing before. He ran his finger down the barrel, stroked it. Who'd have thought it, him, the old farmer from Bussex Drove, sat in a ditch a few yards from the new king, a pistol in his hand? It was an odd thing, life.

He traced the shape inside the handle. Beautifully made, this pistol. Real workmanship. Took skill to make that. He held it in his hand. Counted to three and aimed. Smiled. What a thing to have in his hand. He rested it in his lap, then lifted and aimed it as fast as he could.

Not fast enough.

He did it again. There, that was faster. He liked this, it was better than haymaking, even.

The man put his spyglass down and stretched his hand out for the pistol. The farmer lifted it and aimed it as quickly as he could: one last time, for it wasn't every day you got to hold something like that.

Lift and aim. Finger on the hook. And. Pull.

The gun went off and black smoke filled the air. A silence while the sound settled in their ears, then the noise of the opposing army, the king's men, as they began their attack.

The farmer's wife and her sister stayed at the farm. They sat up all night and ran from window to door to table, listening to the guns and the screams.

At dawn the sister packed a basket of cakes and covered them with a cloth. She let herself out of the house in silence, so as not to wake the wife who slept in her husband's favourite chair.

Stepped out into the misty morning and started walking down the drove towards the scene of the battle.

She heard the moaning first, crying and moaning and calling, men and horses. She turned right down the next drove and made her way through the dead bodies, hundreds of them, the fields full of blood. Blood pouring into the rhynes and filling them. Blood spilling over the bars of the gate. She walked round, handing out her cakes to any men who were still conscious.

She found her sister's husband lying where he'd fired the pistol, on the edge of the rhyne. He was alive but unmoving, his eyes closed. She nudged his shoulder and he looked up, saw her there with her basket of cakes.

'Come on,' she said. 'Let's get you back.'

The farmer stood and followed her back through the lake of blood, back along the drove full of moaning soldiers, and back to the house.

He looked at the fire burning in the fireplace and sat down in his comfy chair. He stretched out his feet and listened to the flames, listened to the whispering of the kettle.

'So,' his wife said, 'it's all over.'

'Looks like it.'

'And you survived.'

'I did.'

The next morning the farmer was called out to help dig graves. They cleared grass and topsoil and dug deep down into the earth. They tipped hundreds of bodies in. Soldiers, horses, the odd dog even.

They stopped that evening, for a rest. The farmer stuck his spade into the soil and rubbed the small of his back. He looked around the moors. 'Where's Monmouth?'

The man digging with him paused. 'Buggered off.'

'Ah,' the farmer said.

'Soon as he saw he'd lost. Soon as that daft sod let the pistol off.'

'Ah,' the farmer said. A pause. 'Well, least the weather's gone our way.' He laughed. 'You wouldn't wanna be doing this in the lashing rain.'

When they had finished burying the dead, the living rebels were despatched in the Bloody Assizes: to gaol, to faraway countries, to naked deaths chained to the gallows on the road to Bridgwater.

One night, when Judge Jeffreys had returned home and daily life began again, the farmer came back from checking his animals and found the two sisters had rearranged the room. There, in front of the fire, were three chairs. The farmer sat in his normal place, the two sisters either side. There they sat with the bubbling of flame and kettle. Now and again one or other of them spoke.

'It was a terrible night,' the wife said.

A long pause.

'A terrible night,' the sister agreed.

And then, after a while, the sister stood up and walked to the table, came back with a wooden platter. A pile of rich, y ow cakes. She held the platter out to the farmer's wife. Then to the farmer. 'Here, have a cake,' the sister said.

'Do you know,' the farmer said, 'I think I might. See, they do look good.'

The sister smiled and the farmer took a cake and ate it, then another. They really were quite delicious.

So there they sat, the three of them, with their cakes and their thoughts. The farmer finished his third cake, brushed the crumbs from his lap and closed his eyes. He slipped in and out of sleep and dreamed of the five attempts it took to remove Monmouth's head, imagining how that would feel, to have the blade cleave away under your chin.

And he dreamed of his land, how the grass would be long and green, fed by the blood and bodies in the earth, in this, the last battle to take place on English soil.

And he dreamed of how his milk would be the creamiest, richest milk in Somerset.

~

Iris walked to the memorial stone. 'They're buried down here? All those men?'

'The ones who died down here are,' Father said. 'They sent some away to other countries.' He took a small flagon from the basket and pulled out the cork. Drank the cider. Passed it to Frank.

'Was it really the last battle in England?' Frank asked. He offered the flagon to Iris but she shook her head.

'It was,' Father said, 'and if you come here on the night of July 6th, you can hear the men, riding across the moors. Crying for help.'

Father took the flagon, replaced the cork and put it back in the basket.

'You ever come to see if you can hear them?' Frank asked.

'Not sure I'd want to,' Father said.

'Are they ghosts?'

'Must be, eh?'

They sat in silence for a while, then Iris spoke. 'It's not a funny story. All those people dying.'

'It was a long time ago,' Father said.

Two cows in the opposite field moved through the grass, up to the edge of the rhyne. Stared at them.

'There's bodies buried everywhere,' Iris said.

'There would be,' Father said. 'People die.'

'There's Joseph, Arthur, Merlin in the gold coffin.'

'She's been trying to find the gold coffin,' Frank said.

'Shut up.'

'She has. She's been digging.'

'Shut up,' Iris shouted. 'It's just a game.'

One cow shook her head and blew through her nostrils, the sound loud on the quiet moors.

'There's one game I don't like.'

'You wanna shut up, Frank,' Iris warned.

'Steady,' Father said.

'But I don't.'

'I said, shut up.' Iris stared at Frank and he looked down at the grass.

'What is it?' Father asked.

'Nothing,' Frank said.

Father shook his head. 'Sit and eat summat for God's sake, Iris.'

Iris looked round, at the four stones and the trees. At Frank and Father on the grass.

The cows watched, their tails moving.

Silence.

Iris sat down and Father picked up his knife. Pushed the blade into the earth to clean it, wiped it on the grass. He took an apple and sliced it in half.

That evening, after Frank had undressed and climbed into bed, Mother came in. Sat down.

'You're up,' Frank said.

'That's right.'

'You still tired?'

She smiled. 'No. I'm all right now.'

'What's she gonna be called?'

Mother shrugged. 'Still ain't come to us.'

Frank yawned.

'You ready for sleep?'

'No.'

'You're worn out,' she said. 'Ain't used to a day out.'

Frank lay back against the pillow. Mother leant forward and stroked his hair. 'You enjoyed it though?'

Frank nodded.

'He tell you the story?'

'All those fields,' Frank said. 'Full of blood.'

'Don't be thinking about the blood.'

'Can't help it.'

'He ought to leave them bits out. Enough to keep you awake.'

'You stay here till I'm asleep?' Frank asked.

'Soft bugger. Cos of the story?'

Frank shook his head.

'Cos of the baby?'

Frank smiled. 'I like the baby.'

'I know you do.'

Mother stood up. Patted him on the shoulder. 'Come on, sleep.'

She walked to the door, looked back at him, then left.

Later that night, in bed in the hot room. The window open and the air still.

Frank woke, stretched his leg across the bed, felt the empty space.

He sat up. Listened. Nothing.

He pulled on his clothes and crept quietly downstairs. The

back door was open and he went out in bare feet. Stood for a few minutes until his eyes adjusted to the dark.

She sat on the flagstones, leaning back against the wall of the house, a willow stick in her hand, drawing shapes on the ground. Frank watched her and after a few minutes walked over, sat down next to her. The flagstones were cooler now.

'I couldn't sleep,' she whispered.

Frank looked up at the black sky. The far-off cry of an owl.

'Frank,' Iris said.

'What?'

'Those fields we were in today. They were red.'

'Green,' Frank said. 'They were green.'

'I keep seeing them in all different colours,' Iris said. 'Silver from the floods. Yellow from kingcups and irises. Red from the blood.'

'They were green.'

'I was thinking, before you came out. I was sat here thinking of that night with the stars.'

Frank yawned. He tucked his knees up and wrapped his arms round his legs.

'You know what he said, don't you?'

'I dunno what you're talking about,' Frank said.

'Father. He said if it was still and quiet enough, God'd come and walk the earth.'

'D'you reckon he would?' Frank asked.

Iris thought a second. 'Yeh, I do.'

'Reckon he can walk?'

'Dunno how else he'd get about.'

'What d'you reckon he looks like?'

'I don't know.' Iris yawned.

'You shouldn't be out,' Frank said.

'I'll be all right.'

'Mother wouldn't let you out.'

'She doesn't know.'

They sat in silence a while, then Iris spoke. 'I know what I'd ask God.'

Frank waited.

'I'd ask him about what happens when you die.'

'You die when you die,' Frank said.

'No you don't.'

'Course you do.'

'No.' Iris hit the stick on the ground. 'Think about it,' she said. 'There's Jesus on the cross, how did he live again?'

'I don't know. Did the robin do it?'

'He didn't make him live again. He'd have done that anyway.'

'Maybe Jesus is the only one who can live again after he's died.'

'What about the soldiers from the battle? Riding their horses on the moors.'

'Maybe it was just a story,' Frank said. 'Maybe the battle happened but the ghosts don't come.'

Iris turned and looked at Frank. 'And King Arthur lying there, waiting.'

'I don't know.'

'Will you come to the house?'

Frank shook his head. 'Not now.'

'You ain't told no one about it?'

'No.'

'Good.'

'What I don't understand,' Frank said, 'is why you keep going there in the nights.'

'Come with me now and I'll show you.'

'I don't like the nights.'

'Are you scared?'

'Course not. S'just you can't see.'

'I got candles.'

'I don't want to go.'

Iris stood up. She stretched her arms out to the sides, the willow stick in her hand. 'Stand like this.'

'Why?'

'Just do it.'

Frank stood and stretched out his arms.

'You can feel it,' she said. 'How it must've been when he was on the cross.'

'I've had enough of the games.' Frank let his arms drop. 'I want to go in.'

'Don't go.' Iris took his arm, pulled him.

'I'm not going to the house,' Frank said.

'I'm not taking you to the house.' She led him to the bare patch of earth by the hedge. 'Watch this.' She raised the stick then drove it down into the earth. 'It'll grow,' she said. 'Like the Holy Thorn.'

Frank turned away.

'You do believe me, don't you?'

Frank said nothing.

'Tell me you believe me.'

'It's just games.' Frank looked back at the house, the shape of it in the dark.

Iris bent close to Frank's face. 'You do believe me. About that and the baby.'

Frank shook his head. 'There's only one baby. That baby in there.' He pointed at the house.

'You'll see, Frank, when I have my baby.' Iris gripped Frank's arm again and he pulled back.

'You're hurting me.'

'Good. Don't you dare tell anyone. Any of it.'

'I ain't told no one.'

Iris let him go and he ran towards the house, stopped just

before the door. Rubbed his sore arm. Watched her walk round the corner of the house and out of sight.

~

'Iris.'

No answer.

'Iris.'

Margaret ran in. She turned on the light and sat beside him in her nightdress. Took his hand in hers. 'It's all right,' she said. 'I'm here.'

Frank lifted up his head and looked at her. 'You're here, Iris. You're here.'

The door opened and George came in.

'It's all right, George,' Margaret said. 'You can go back to bed.'

George ignored her. 'Hello, Dad.' He sat on the second chair.

'Go on,' Margaret said. 'Back to bed.'

'Iris,' Frank shouted.

'Sshh,' Margaret whispered.

'Who's Iris?'

'Please, George. Go on back.'

'No.'

Frank pulled his hand away from Margaret. 'I had to clear the rhynes out after,' he said.

'What's he saying?' George said.

'I'd cut the heads off the irises and throw them in the water.'

'He's confused,' Margaret said.

George rubbed his hair, hit his head with an open palm. 'Dad.'

'Iris.'

'Why's he call you Iris?'

'It's all right,' Margaret said.

165

'Stay there, Iris.'

'It's all right,' she said. 'I won't go anywhere.'

Frank closed his eyes.

A field full of yellow flowers. Flag irises. Kingcups. Lady's smock. Yellow rattle. Meadowsweet. As he walked through them, the flowers got bigger and he got smaller until he couldn't see over them. The sun came down through the petals and the light was yellow. The green stems were trees and he climbed a blade of grass and walked along it, careful not to cut his bare feet on the sharp fold running down its centre.

He looked up at the greens and the yellows. The blue of the sky beyond. The dark grey clouds moving towards each other. He smelled the peat and the dry grass and then he heard thunder and felt the water on his face.

'Dad.' Margaret wiped Frank's face.

Frank opened his eyes: Margaret with a tissue in her hand; George next to her, leaning forward.

'You all right, Dad?' George asked.

Frank shook his head.

Silence while Frank looked around him, at Margaret and George. Margaret stood up, placed her hand on George's back. 'Come on, love, back to bed. Let Dad sleep.' George followed her to the door.

When he'd gone, Margaret came back and sat down. 'You okay?' she asked quietly.

Frank nodded gently. 'Is it morning?'

Margaret looked at her watch. 'Half four.'

Frank stroked the counterpane. 'Is the fire out?'

Margaret looked over. 'Just about. You want me to put more coal on?'

Frank shook his head. 'Margaret.'

'What?'

'I don't want any more morphine.'

Margaret reached out and touched the drip. 'That's fine,' she said. 'If that's what you want.'

'It's what I want.' He turned his face away.

They sat in silence for a long time, then Frank spoke. 'I could have told them.'

Margaret waited.

'I could. I could have told them everything.'

Margaret sat, dead still.

'But I didn't.' Frank cleared his throat. 'And then later,' he said, 'later when I thought I'd forgotten it all, I had you.'

'Me?'

Frank stared at the window, stared hard.

'Yes, you. You see, you looked like her. When you were a girl.'

'Iris?'

Frank nodded.

Margaret thought for a while. 'I see,' she said.

Blue Lias

Early morning. Frank opened his eyes: four squares of glass; light and shade on the white walls; wooden floorboards.

He turned.

Iris was on her back, sleeping, eyes closed, mouth slightly open. Her dark hair on the white of the pillow.

In the night, outside, the stick in the earth and the feel of her hand gripping him, hurting him. He shook his head.

The smell of fresh bread from downstairs.

He got out of bed, ran down the stairs.

She stood by the open oven door. Sliding out the tin.

'You made some bread?'

She laughed. 'It ain't cooled yet.'

'Just one slice.'

'It'll ruin it.'

'Please.'

'Go on then. Just this once.' She stood at the table and tipped out the hot loaf. Cut off the crust, passed it to Frank. Steam and the soft inside. He spread on some butter and bit into it.

'Thought the smell'd get you up.'

She removed the net from the milk jug and poured milk into two cups. Added tea. 'Sleep all right?'

Frank nodded. 'Where's the baby?'

'Upstairs.'

'Ain't she coming down?'

'I'll get her when she wakes. They sleep a lot.' She passed a cup to Frank. 'You all done a good job while I was in bed,' she said, turning back to the fire, breaking the turves with the poker to let it die down. 'Where's Iris?'

Frank shrugged.

'She's not still sleeping?'

Frank looked up.

'Iris. I said she's not still sleeping? Must've worn her out, yesterday.'

Frank shrugged again.

Mother walked to the stairs, called Iris's name, told her to get up.

Frank looked down at his tea. A bubble of cream rose up and burst into an oily ball of fat, floating on the hot liquid.

'You're quiet today.'

'Bit.' Frank poked at the fat with his finger and it disappeared, then resurfaced.

'Spose you'd like more bread.'

'Can I?'

'Just for you.' She cut him another slice.

They heard the door close upstairs and Iris came down, already dressed, sat at the table. Half asleep still.

'You all right?' Mother asked.

'Yeh.'

She passed Iris a slice of bread. 'Still warm.'

'Any tea?'

Mother poured another cup and passed it to her. Sat down and cut a slice of bread for herself.

'I was wondering,' Iris said, 'if you got a name yet for the baby.'

'Not yet.'

'When you gonna get one?'

'One'll come when we know what she's like.'

'She asleep?'

'Yeh. Upstairs,' Mother smiled at Iris. 'See, I told you you'd come round.'

Father stood outside in the sun, by the vegetables. He pulled two carrots from the black earth, wiped them on the grass and gave them to Iris and Frank. 'Better get to work.'

They walked over the sleeper bridge and started across the grass. Walked till they reached the cutting field, the men and women working.

Ruckles, hyles and winrows.

Black turves.

Green grass and dark soil, blue sky and water in the rhynes. Long willow leaves. Dead irises and velvet bulrushes. Dragon-flies on the rhynes. And in the grass, flat white yarrow heads. Purple clover heads. Red campion.

Later, tired, they walked back across the fields and past the allotment, to the house. Mother stood in the doorway, the baby in her arms. A pile of brown feathers outside the back door.

Father filled the bucket from the well and poured the water into the bowl in the scullery. They washed, cooled their skin and sat outside in the shade from the dying sun, in the thick, hot air.

Mother joined them, the baby put down to sleep upstairs.

'You hungry?'

'Starving,' Father said.

'Good.' Mother fetched plates for them. Chicken, the juices poured on. Potatoes in their skins. Runners and carrots from the garden.

They ate in silence, taking every piece of flesh and skin off the bones. Pressing the potatoes into the juices. Father finished first. 'God, that was good.' He smiled. 'What's for pudding?'

Mother laughed. She stood up, took some of the dirty dishes in, came back with a cake.

'Reckoned you'd make summat.'

'Yeh, well.' Mother looked at Frank's empty plate. 'You ain't eaten all that?'

Frank grinned. 'I been working.'

'You'll be bigger than your father if you carry on like that.'

'Better not be,' Father said.

Mother cut the cake into slices and handed them out. They ate from their hands and let the crumbs fall onto the grass.

The blue of the sky deepened slowly and birds flew in circles high above. The cow lifted her head and called out. 'Better get on to bed soon, Frank,' Mother said. 'If you're working tomorrow.'

'He's all right.'

The baby woke upstairs, her cries clear through the open window.

'She's got you working hard,' Father said.

Mother smiled and went in. Came out carrying the baby in her shawl. She sat and held her. 'You ain't having your milk till later, got to get some sleep. You're wearing us out.' She looked up at Iris. 'You wanna hold her, Iris?'

Iris nodded.

Mother placed the baby in Iris's arms, kneeling on the grass beside them. 'You all right?'

Iris nodded and Father smiled.

They stayed there a while, then Iris said, 'Take her back.'

'Don't you like her?'

'Ain't that. I'm just not used to it. You know, not used to holding her and that.'

Mother took the baby from Iris's arms. 'Bit of practice, you'll get used to it.'

'Course I will.'

Mother sighed. 'We ought to be going on in.'

'There's one thing,' Iris said.

'What's that?'

'It's just, I was wondering. D'you reckon she could stay in our room, just for tonight?'

'I have to get up in the night, feed her, love.'

'I could bring her to you, you know, when she cries.'

'I don't know,' Mother said.

'Please. It'd help me get used to her.'

Mother looked at Father, who leaned back against the wall, eyes closed.

'Soon as she cries, I'll bring her. Or I'll get you.'

Mother shrugged.

'She is my sister.'

Mother nodded. 'All right, then. Don't spose there's any harm. Long as you get me straight away.'

'I will.'

Mother patted the baby's back. 'I'll go and feed her now, then, move the crib in.'

She walked into the house.

~

Frank, in the dark room. In the night. The dark shapes: the chest and the chair; the end of the bedstead.

He reached down and patted the bed, felt for the tube and found the button. He held it in his hand as the pain climbed.

He shifted his weight in the bed, felt the counterpane with the fingertips of his other hand. The spaces between the candlewick tufts, the curves of them. He took his finger off the button. Let it go.

No more morphine. No more memory.

175

All he wanted was to stop it, to have the blackness of a moonless and clouded night inside his head.

～

Dawn: the black became deep grey and the birds began to cry out the new day. Frank turned in bed, threw out an arm. Nothing there. He opened his eyes, waited for the shapes in the room to be clear. The window, the chest and chair. The crib at the end of the bedstead.

The baby.

He sat up.

Stepped onto the warm wooden floorboards and walked over to the crib. Bent over and looked inside. Nothing.

He walked to the door. Opened it. Stood on the dark landing, then felt for his mother's door, lifted the latch and went in.

Walked round her side of the bed to where her pillows were, where her head lay. He reached out and touched her hair.

She woke up straightaway. Sat up. 'She need feeding?'

'It's me, Frank.'

'Where's the baby?'

'I don't know.'

She sat up. 'What d'you mean? Where is she?' She pulled roughly at Father's shoulder. 'Wake up.' She got out of bed and ran to the door. Ran the few steps into Frank and Iris's room. To the crib at the foot of the bed.

'Where's my baby?'

'I don't know,' Frank said.

'My baby.' Shouting now. 'Where's Iris?'

'I don't know,' Frank said.

Father came in. The shapes of them in the dark. The shape of the empty crib. 'What's going on?'

176

Mother took Frank by the arms. 'Where is she?' She shook him, hard. 'You must know.'

Frank pulled away.

'It's all right,' Father said. He bent down, spoke quietly to Frank. 'D'you know where she could be?'

Frank nodded. 'I think so.'

Frank and Father ran from the house into the grey dawn world. Along the drove. Past the cutting field. Past the bridge where the drove crossed the river. Climbed a gate and ran through fields, jumping the rhynes, until they reached the next drove. Ran along to the orchard.

They jumped down from the gate into the long grass. Through the trees to the house.

The door was closed, caught on the flagstones. Father used his shoulder to push until the door gave and opened. They stood in the doorway and listened. Nothing. Frank looked around. Broken glass on the draining board, one of the glass jars from the shelf.

Next to the pieces of glass there were stems and roots of plants. Tiny fragments of bright green, from the rhynes, from the roots of bulrushes and irises.

The door into the next room was closed and Father turned the handle slowly and opened it.

The fireplace full of ash. The curtains still at the window, but the tin bath gone. Just the bare beaten earth floor.

And what Iris had done.

In the centre of the room was a group of bleached bones, laid out in the shape of the animal they had once been. Long yellow teeth in the skull. Surrounding that was a circle of bulrushes, the brown velvet heads in the centre facing inwards, the frayed stems pointing out towards the walls of the room.

Between each of the bulrushes were yellow flag irises, their petals wilting into the earth floor.

And around this circle, other collections. A pile of blue and white china, laid in a mosaic oval, each fragment a tiny distance from the next. Glass in different colours, laid in squares. Brown earthenware shards in a line stretching along the wall under the window.

More bones, long and thin, laid out in stars, placed on top of each other.

Flower heads, cut from their stems, in the shapes of other flowers. Small red crab apples in spirals.

And clusters of dead butterflies, vivid and faded: marbled whites, common blues, small coppers, orange tips. Peacocks and tortoiseshells.

Father stood and stared at the patterns. Frank stepped over them to the fire, reached out his hand. Cold ash. He picked up the top turf from the pile. It was dry, light. Threads of rotted leaves and stems. He put it back. Looked back at the open door into the scullery, at the broken glass on the draining board. Took a deep breath and walked over to the closed door leading into the bedroom.

Father followed.

The door opened slowly. The room beyond, the opening in the roof up to the grey morning sky, the bedstead with the sacking on it. The reed scattered. The one child's boot on the earth floor.

The bed of reed under the window.

And Iris.

Iris, in the dawn light, in the reed bed.

Her head down.

178

Legs outstretched. Bare, white legs.

The straps of her dress pulled down. One swollen pink breast.

And the baby at the other breast.

Father's voice breaking the silence. 'What are you doing?'

And Iris looking up. 'Feeding my baby.'

Father stepping closer, hands outstretched. 'Give her to me.'

Iris pulling the baby closer to her chest. 'No.'

Father stepping closer still. One small, slow step.

The quiet of the room. The grey sky above.

His voice gentle: 'Let me hold her. I'll give her back after.'

Iris's head still shaking. 'She hasn't finished.'

'I'll give her back to you.'

Her head shaking. 'No.'

'Come on.'

Another small step closer and his arms stretched out, waiting.

'You can have her back. I promise.'

And Iris looking, staring, then nodding. Relaxing her hold, moving the baby away from her body. Her two pink swollen breasts. The baby held out.

Father reaching out and the baby moving from her arms to his.

The baby's body, passed to him.

Her white wax skin thickening and still.

The sucking blister on her lips. Pale blue lips.

Her cold body.

Cold, cold body.

Father looking down at her in his arms and his voice, different now. 'What have you done?'

And Iris, standing up, the dry reed moving across the earth floor. Iris and her bare feet, stepping back, away from him. Hooking up the straps of her dress, covering her breasts.

'She was crying,' Iris said. 'Crying and wouldn't stop, even when I fed her.'

Frank saw the baby's hand hanging down. Her fingers bone-white. The beds of her nails blue.

Father, looking down at the baby in his arms.

'I just stopped her crying. That's all. Just stopped her.'

'You stopped her breathing.'

Iris, taking another step back. 'She'll be all right. The others were.'

'What others?'

'In the stories. Jesus, after the cross.'

Father's terrible, terrible voice: 'No.'

Iris staring at Frank. 'I told you.'

Frank moving backwards, towards the door.

'I said I was having a baby. And you didn't believe me.'

Frank looking at Father.

Father's head down, the baby's still body in his arms.

Dawn and the first touches of the sun. Reaching in through the dusty glass.

Lighting up the scene.

The maiden mother, untouched. The manger of straw. The new infant.

~

Silence in the room.

Frank looked at the window. The first light and the birds singing. Dawn coming.

The sound of a tap from downstairs.

So.

There it was.

None of it forgotten.

*

Frank closed his eyes.

Slept.

Later Margaret stood, stretched, rubbed the small of her back where she'd been sitting so long.

The rain was stopping now.

She sat back down. Looked at Frank in the bed.

Eyes closed.

She bent down and poured the last of the lukewarm tea.

'Is it morning?'

'I thought you were asleep.'

'I was.'

'I didn't wake you, did I?'

'No.'

Frank watched her for a while, watched her play with her wedding ring. Push her hair behind her ears.

'I know I shouldn't have come in,' she said, 'but I couldn't sleep, just wanted to sit here.'

'S'all right.'

'You got some sleep, then.'

'A bit, just now.'

Margaret picked up her tea. 'D'you want me to make a fresh pot?'

Frank shook his head.

Margaret sipped. 'I was thinking,' she said, 'when you were sleeping, about how I used to wake in the nights. I'd lie in bed in there,' she gestured towards the other room, 'and think the whole world was asleep and it was just me awake.' She looked at Frank.

He lay, still.

'Some nights I remember I'd come in here to you and Mum. One night you were both asleep and I tiptoed over and looked in the crib. It wasn't long after George was born.'

Frank could see the sky, through the window, lighter now.

Margaret smiled. 'I loved him when he was a baby. Used to sit and wait for hours, wait for him to wake up so I could hold him. You used to tell me to leave him alone. You hated me holding him.'

Frank nodded.

'I never understood that.'

'No.'

Margaret shrugged. 'Anyway, it's all gone now.' She laughed. 'He ain't a baby any more.'

'No.'

'I know you don't want me to say this, but he'll be all right, Dad.'

Silence.

'Me and Brian talked about it. We'll move in. He won't have to go anywhere. He can stay here.'

Frank stared at the crack in the ceiling.

Margaret finished her tea and put the cup back on the tray.

Another silence, then Frank spoke quietly. 'When you move in.'

Margaret waited.

Frank nodded towards the window. 'You mustn't cut the tree down.'

Margaret gazed out into the deep grey morning. 'I won't.'

'You promise me?'

'I promise.'

The two of them in the room and the tree outside.

Eventually, 'Why that tree?'

'Iris grew it,' Frank said.

'Did she?'

'She didn't know she did. She stuck a stick in the ground one night and it grew. That's all.'

'Oh,' Margaret said.

A pause then, 'What time is it now?'

Margaret angled her wrist towards the light. 'Nearly eight.'

'Has the rain stopped?' Frank asked.

'No. Looks like it might have slowed a bit, mind.' She cleared her throat. 'I wanted to ask you something.'

A pause.

'About Iris.'

Frank closed his eyes.

'I just wondered why you hadn't said anything before. You know.'

Nothing.

'I mean, I just wondered.'

Frank turned and looked at Margaret. He looked at her and said nothing.

'No,' she said. She pushed her hair behind her ears again.

Frank's gaze dropped to the covers, to his hands lying there.

'I'm sorry,' she said. 'I shouldn't have asked.'

Frank shrugged and they stayed like that for a while.

Then: 'It was a long time ago.'

Margaret nodded slowly.

'All a long time ago.'

'You haven't told me what happened to her.'

'No,' Frank said. 'I know.'

Another silence.

'She wasn't well. You know.'

'Ill?'

Frank shrugged. 'In the head, I spose.'

'Was she taken away?'

He nodded.

Then nothing.

Until: 'D'you think George is up yet?'

'You want to see him?' Margaret asked.

Frank nodded. 'That'd be good.'

'I'll go and see. You want me to wake him if he's asleep?'

'Yeh.'

Margaret stood up. 'Spose it's time he was up anyway.' She picked up the tray, balancing it on one hip while she opened the door. She looked back at Frank, then left the room.

George rubbed his eyes. 'Is it morning?'

'It is.'

George nodded. 'Margaret said it was. I had a good sleep. I needed that.'

'Yeh. Spec you did.' Frank closed his eyes.

'You going to sleep?'

He shook his head. 'Hurts.'

'Oh,' George said. 'Hurts, does it?'

'A bit,' Frank said. 'George, you open the window for me?'

'Again?' George asked. 'I done that before.' But he shrugged and stood up. Pushed at the frame so the window swung wide open and fresh air filled the room.

Frank looked at the tree. The pale grey sky. Listened to the birds, clearer now. Louder.

George sat back down. 'You know I said I'd like to be a boat?'

Frank smiled. 'Yeh.'

'There's summat else I'd like to be.'

'George.'

'See, if I could be an animal who could talk . . .'

'George.'

'Yeh.'

'You don't remember your mother.'

George looked at Frank. 'How do you know that?'

'You told me, George.'

'I don't remember saying that. When did I say it?'

'Doesn't matter when you said it.'

184

'Did I say it yesterda...

'Maybe.'

'Was yesterday the day y...

...doesn't matter when you...me?'

...orge nodded. 'Funny I don...st listen...ther,' he

...aid. 'You...remember everything, G...that sle...

'...urse I wi...bed his eyes again...ber me.'

'And no one can stay h...ever.'

'In this room?'

'No. I mean in life.'

George laughed. 'You wouldn't want to...

Frank thought for a second. 'No.'

'Bored,' George said. 'You'd get bored.'

'I spose you would.'

George stood up and crossed the room to...el in front of the fire. Picked up the small dustpan and b...h and started sweeping the ashes from the hearth into the...ate. 'Make a terrible mess, fires,' he said.

'Listen to me.'

George looked around.

'You got Margaret,' Frank said.

'I have.'

'And there's Brian. You like Brian.'

A pause. Then, 'Are you going somewhere?'

'Not right now, George, but one day.'

George thought. 'And I'll live with Margaret and Brian?'

'That's right.'

'Where?'

'Here.'

George nodded slowly. He finished sweeping and put the

brush and pan near...side. His knees clicked as he stood up, ...over to lean on the bedstead.

'Dad,' he said...

'Yeh.'

A lon...

'D...'

'...ell,' G... said, 'it's these p...ey keep slipp...'

...own.

'Ah...'

'D'you ... the elastic's ...one?'

'I du...' Frank shr...ged. 'Elastic does go. In the end.'

George ...ght for a second.

'May...b...garet'll sort them for you.'

'I'll ask... shall I?'

Frank ...red. 'You do that.'

George ...pped his hands and rubbed his hair.

'So you ...all right?'

'Yeh.'

'And you...l be all right?'

George frowned. 'Yeh. Bit hungry, mind.' He walked to the door. 'I'll go and see Margaret, see if she'll make me a breakfast.' He opened the door. Smiled at Frank, and left the room.

The open window with the grey sky. The birds and the tree outside. The white walls. Chest. Bedsteads. Chairs. Wooden floor.

Frank lay back, settling deep into the pillows. Closed his eyes.

Lay in the silence of the room.